A Book of Nature Poems

OTHER BOOKS BY WILLIAM COLE

A Book of Love Poems

D. H. Lawrence:
Poems Selected for Young People

Oh, What Nonsense!

The Sea, Ships, and Sailors

A Book of
Nature Poems

Selected by WILLIAM COLE

Illustrated by Robert Andrew Parker

The Viking Press   *New York*

808.81   1. Poetry—Collections
2. Nature poetry

Acknowledgment is made to The New Yorker Magazine, Inc., for permission to
reprint the following poems copyright by them: "Apples in New Hampshire," by
Marie Gilchrist, Copyright 1932, © 1960 The New Yorker Magazine, Inc. "Noc-
turne," by Frances Frost, Copyright 1934, © 1962 The New Yorker Magazine, Inc.
"Winter Morning," by William Jay Smith, Copyright © 1967 The New Yorker
Magazine, Inc. "The Big Nasturtiums," by Robert Beverly Hale, Copyright 1951
The New Yorker Magazine, Inc. "Cider Song," by Mildred Weston, Copyright 1931,
© 1959 The New Yorker Magazine, Inc. "Echo," by Mildred Weston, Copyright
1931, © 1959 The New Yorker Magazine, Inc. All reprinted by permission of The
New Yorker Magazine, Inc.

Additional acknowledgments on pages 254 through 256 constitute an extension
of this copyright page.

Contents

Introduction

The two great subjects for poets are love and nature; and in sheer quantity, poems about nature win out. Much of the stuff that appears on the editorial pages of daily newspapers is about the first robin of spring or the poor defenseless dandelion or the babbling brook. Poets churn out this "newspaper verse," as it is called, by the yard. *Nature* is a huge, huge word, which can include everything in the universe. For the purposes of this book, the word refers to everything not man-made—and, as I put it to one poet, without a beating heart.

Every worthwhile anthology is extremely personal. I have read thousands of nature poems, looking for those I wanted to include in this book. Even so, I can't call this the definitive book of nature poetry. I'm sure that there are some great poems that have been left out—they simply didn't hit me. I have included some very familiar poems because I like them, and I have excluded other very familiar poems (such as Joyce Kilmer's "Trees") because I *don't* like them.

I can't think of any great poet, with the exception of W. S. Gilbert, who hasn't written about nature. There are some poets who write about little else. I think particularly of the English poets John Clare and William Barnes—two men whose genius is seldom appreciated. Clare, who died more than a hundred years ago, spent most of his youth roaming the fields and lived in amazingly close communication with the things of nature. Barnes, who lived at roughly the same time, was a native of Dorset, and he found it natural to write most of his poems in the dialect of that part of England. It *looks* difficult, but if you read it aloud, the meaning will come through. Take the phrase "An' vishes scealy zides did gleare," which is puzzling at first glance but when said aloud turns out to be "And fishes' scaly sides did glare."

I have not made any conscious effort to balance things—to have so many summer poems and so many winter poems, and the same number about trees as there are about flowers. I simply went through a couple of large libraries of poetry and chose what I considered the most effective nature poems, and the balance seemed to take care of itself. It did turn out, however, that poets show certain preferences, or perhaps it is that they just naturally write better poems about some subjects. The moon, for example—poets are mad about the moon. And snow—they love it. On the other hand, I didn't come across one poem about deserts; come to think of it, I guess that makes sense. I see that there are two poems about mushrooms; this may seem odd, when there are also only two poems about mountains, but I happened to like the mushroom poems I found better than most of the mountain poems. And anyhow, who's to say that mountains are more important than mushrooms?

The English have always produced the most, and the best, poetry about nature. Perhaps this is because their island is so small, and each inch of land is treasured. The poets of the United States, Australia, and Canada write more frequently about large vistas; they'll write about a prairie while the English poet writes about a single daisy. Personally, I prefer the English view; I'd rather be on intimate terms with a lovely brook than look at the Grand Canyon (which is, after all, as a visiting Englishman described it, only "an interesting hole"). I don't like "nature trails" where everything is labeled. There are no surprises there, no personal communication with nature. I could never go for tourist sights—such things have been "looked out," as D. H. Lawrence puts it. There is nothing more soothing than a walk in a good woods; it is fascinating to see what weather and vines have done to a fallen tree, to be the first to come upon one of nature's phenomena. Give me the small majesties that I can feel are my own—the tiny perfect wild-flowers on the forest floor, the surprise of mushrooms, the way a tree announces rain. Other people can have their gaudy sunsets—I think they're in quite bad taste. I go along with John Clare, who wrote in a letter to his son, "I met with birds bees trees flowers all talked to me louder than the busy hum of men."

William Cole

from **Childe Harold's Pilgrimage**

Are not the mountains, waves, and skies, a part
Of me and of my soul, as I of them?
Is not the love of these deep in my heart
With a pure passion?

GEORGE GORDON, LORD BYRON

O Feel the Gentle Air

Spring and Blossoming

The First Spring Morning

Look! Look! the spring is come:
 O feel the gentle air,
That wanders thro' the boughs to burst
 The thick buds everywhere!
 The birds are glad to see
 The high unclouded sun:
Winter is fled away, they sing,
 The gay time is begun.

Adown the meadows green
 Let us go dance and play,
And look for violets in the lane,
 And ramble far away
 To gather primroses,
 That in the woodlands grow,
And hunt for oxlips, or if yet
 The blades of bluebells show.

There the old woodman gruff
 Hath half the coppice cut,
And weaves the hurdles all day long
 Beside his willow hut.
 We'll steal on him, and then
 Startle him, all with glee
Singing our song of winter fled
 And summer soon to be.

ROBERT BRIDGES

15

Spring Quiet

Gone were but the Winter,
 Come were but the Spring,
I would go to a covert
 Where the birds sing.

Where in the whitethorn
 Singeth a thrush,
And a robin sings
 In the holly-bush.

Full of fresh scents
 Are the budding boughs
Arching high over
 A cool green house:

Full of sweet scents
 And whispering air
Which sayeth softly:
 "We spread no snare;

Here dwell in safety,
 Here dwell alone,
With a clear stream
 And a mossy stone.

Here the sun shineth
 Most shadily;
Here is heard an echo
 Of the far sea,
  Though far off it be."

CHRISTINA ROSSETTI

The Spring Will Come

O the Spring will come,
And once again the wind be in the West
Breathing the odor of the sea; and life,
Life that was ugly, and work that had grew a curse,
Be God's best gifts again; and in your heart
You'll find once more the dreams you thought were dead.

H. D. LOWRY

March

Awake to the cold light
of wet wind running
twigs in tremors. Walls
are naked. Twilights raw—
and when the sun taps steeples
their glistenings dwindle
upward . . .

March
slips along the ground
like a mouse under pussy
willows, a little hungry.

The vagrant ghost of winter,
is it this that keeps the chimney
busy still? For something still
nudges shingles and windows:

but waveringly,—this ghost,
this slate-eyed saintly wraith
of winter wanes
and knows its waning.

HART CRANE

To Spring

O thou with dewy locks, who lookest down
Through the clear windows of the morning, turn
Thine angel eyes upon our western isle,
Which in full choir hails thy approach, O Spring!

The hills tell each other, and the listening
Valleys hear; all our longing eyes are turned
Up to thy bright pavilions: issue forth,
And let thy holy feet visit our clime.

Come o'er the eastern hills, and let our winds
Kiss thy perfumed garments; let us taste
Thy morn and evening breath; scatter thy pearls
Upon our love-sick land that mourns for thee.

O deck her forth with thy fair fingers; pour
Thy soft kisses on her bosom; and put
Thy golden crown upon her languished head,
Whose modest tresses were bound up for thee.

WILLIAM BLAKE

Written in March

*While resting on the Bridge
at the Foot of Brother's Water*

The cock is crowing,
The stream is flowing,
The small birds twitter,
The lake doth glitter,
The green field sleeps in the sun;
The oldest and youngest
Are at work with the strongest;
The cattle are grazing,
Their heads never raising;
There are forty feeding like one!

Like an army defeated
The snow hath retreated,
And now doth fare ill
On the top of the bare hill;
The plowboy is whooping—anon—anon:
There's joy in the mountains;
There's life in the fountains;
Small clouds are sailing,
Blue sky prevailing;
The rain is over and gone!

WILLIAM WORDSWORTH

Home-thoughts, from Abroad

Oh, to be in England
Now that April's there,
And whoever wakes in England
Sees, some morning, unaware,
That the lowest boughs and the brushwood sheaf
Round the elm-tree bole are in tiny leaf,
While the chaffinch sings on the orchard bough
In England—now!
And after April, when May follows,
And the whitethroat builds, and all the swallows!
Hark, where my blossomed pear-tree in the hedge
Leans to the field and scatters on the clover
Blossoms and dewdrops—at the bent spray's edge—
That's the wise thrush; he sings each song twice over,
Lest you should think he never could recapture
The first fine careless rapture!
And though the fields look rough with hoary dew,
All will be gay when noontide wakes anew
The buttercups, the little children's dower
—Far brighter than this gaudy melon-flower!

ROBERT BROWNING

In a Spring Still Not Written Of

This morning
with a class of girls outdoors, I saw
how frail poems are
in a world burning up with flowers,
in which, overhead,
the great elms
—green, and tall—
stood carrying leaves in their arms.

The girls listened equally
to my drone, reading, and to the bees'
ricocheting
among them for the blossom on the bone,
or gazed off at a distant mower's
astronomies of green
and clover, flashing,
threshing in the new, untarnished sunlight.

And all the while, dwindling,
tinier, the voices—Yeats, Marvell, Donne—
sank drowning
in a spring still not written of,
as only the sky
clear above the brick bell tower
—blue, and white—
was shifting toward the hour.

Calm, indifferent, cross-legged
or on elbows half-lying in the grass—
how should the great dead
tell them of dying?
They will have time for poems at last,
when they have found they are no more
the beautiful and young
all poems are for.

ROBERT WALLACE

Green Rain

Into the scented woods we'll go,
And see the blackthorn swim in snow.
High above, in the budding leaves,
A brooding dove awakes and grieves;
The glades with mingled music stir,
And wildly laughs the woodpecker.
When blackthorn petals pearl the breeze,
There are the twisted hawthorn trees
Thick-set with buds, as clear and pale
As golden water or green hail—
As if a storm of rain had stood
Enchanted in the thorny wood,
And, hearing fairy voices call,
Hung poised, forgetting how to fall.

MARY WEBB

Spring

Spring, the sweet Spring, is the year's pleasant
        king;
Then blooms each thing, then maids dance in a
        ring,
Cold doth not sting, the pretty birds do sing,
    Cuckoo, jug-jug, pu-we, to-witta-woo!

The palm and may make country houses gay,
Lambs frisk and play, the shepherds pipe all day,
And we hear aye birds tune this merry lay,
    Cuckoo, jug-jug, pu-we, to-witta-woo!

The fields breathe sweet, the daisies kiss our feet,
Young lovers meet, old wives a-sunning sit,
In every street these tunes our ears do greet,
    Cuckoo, jug-jug, pu-we, to-witta-woo!
       Spring! the sweet Spring!

THOMAS NASHE

when faces called flowers float out of the ground
and breathing is wishing and wishing is having—
but keeping is downward and doubting and never
—it's april(yes,april;my darling)it's spring!
yes the pretty birds frolic as spry as can fly
yes the little fish gambol as glad as can be
(yes the mountains are dancing together)

when every leaf opens without any sound
and wishing is having and having is giving—
but keeping is doting and nothing and nonsense
—alive;we're alive,dear:it's (kiss me now)spring!
now the pretty birds hover so she and so he
now the little fish quiver so you and so i
(now the mountains are dancing,the mountains)

when more than was lost has been found has been found
and having is giving and giving is living—
but keeping is darkness and winter and cringing
—it's spring(all our night becomes day)o,it's spring!
all the pretty birds dive to the heart of the sky
and the little fish climb through the mind of the sea
(all the mountains are dancing;are dancing)

e. e. cummings

Song: On May Morning

Now the bright morning star, day's harbinger,
Comes dancing from the east, and leads with her
The flowery May, who from her green lap throws
The yellow cowslip and the pale primrose.
Hail, bounteous May, that does inspire
Mirth and youth and warm desire!
Woods and groves are of thy dressing,
Hill and dale doth boast thy blessing.
Thus we salute thee with our early song,
And welcome thee, and wish thee long.

JOHN MILTON

The Sweet o' the Year

Now the frog, all lean and weak,
Yawning from his famished sleep,
Water in the ditch doth seek,
Fast as he can stretch and leap:
Marshy kingcups burning near,
Tell him 'tis the sweet o' the year.

Now the ant works up his mound
In the moldered piny soil,
And above the busy ground
Takes the joy of earnest toil:
Dropping pine cones, dry and sere,
Warn him 'tis the sweet o' the year.

Now the chrysalis on the wall
Cracks, and out the creature springs,
Raptures in his body small,
Wonders on his dusty wings:
Bells and cups, all shining clear,
Show him 'tis the sweet o' the year.

Now the brown bee, wild and wise,
    Hums abroad, and roves and roams,
Storing in his wealthy thighs
    Treasure for the golden combs:
        Dewy buds and blossoms dear
        Whisper 'tis the sweet o' the year.

Now the merry maids so fair
    Weave the wreaths and choose the queen,
Blooming in the open air,
    Like fresh flowers upon the green;
        Spring, in every thought sincere,
        Thrills them with the sweet o' the year.

Now the lads, all quick and gay,
    Whistle to the browsing herds,
Or in the twilight pastures gray
    Learn the use of whispered words:
        First a blush, and then a tear,
        And then a smile, i' the sweet o' the year.

Now the May fly and the fish
    Play again from noon to night;
Every breeze begets a wish,
    Every motion means delight:
        Heaven high over heath and mere,
        Crowns with blue the sweet o' the year.

Now all Nature is alive,
    Bird and beetle, man and mole;
Beelike goes the human hive,
    Larklike sings the soaring soul:
        Hearty faith and honest cheer
        Welcome in the sweet o' the year.

GEORGE MEREDITH

May 10th

I mean
the fiddleheads have forced their babies,
blind topknots first, up from the thinking rhizomes,
and the shrew's children, twenty to a teaspoon,
breathe to their own astonishment
in the peephole burrow.

I mean
a new bat hangs upside down in the privy;
its eyes are stuck tight, its wrinkled pink mouth twitches,
and in the pond, itself an invented puddle,
tadpoles quake from the jello
and come into being.

I mean walk softly.
The maple's little used-up bells are dropping
and the new leaves are now unpacking,
still wearing their dime-store lacquer,
still cramped and wet from the journey.

MAXINE W. KUMIN

Spring

Nothing is so beautiful as spring—
    When weeds, in wheels, shoot long and lovely and
        lush;
    Thrush's eggs look little low heavens, and thrush
Through the echoing timber does so rinse and wring
The ear, it strikes like lightnings to hear him sing;
    The glassy peartree leaves and blooms, they brush
    The descending blue; that blue is all in a rush
With richness; the racing lambs too have fair their fling.

What is all this juice and all this joy?
    A strain of the earth's sweet being in the beginning
In Eden garden.—Have, get, before it cloy,
    Before it cloud, Christ, lord, and sour with sinning,
Innocent mind and Mayday in girl and boy,
        Most, O maid's child, thy choice and worthy the
            winning.

GERARD MANLEY HOPKINS

The Waking Year

A lady red upon the hill
    Her annual secret keeps;
A lady white within the field
    In placid lily sleeps!

The tidy breezes with their brooms
    Sweep vale, and hill, and tree!
Prithee, my pretty housewives!
    Who may expected be?

The neighbors do not yet suspect!
    The woods exchange a smile,—
Orchard, and buttercup, and bird,
    In such a little while!

And yet how still the landscape stands,
    How nonchalant the wood,
As if the resurrection
    Were nothing very odd!

EMILY DICKINSON

Green Song

The year is round around me now:
groundhog, mouse, and mole climb out,
blind and numb beside their burrow.

Worm and hornet, frog and hornpout,
surface from their sleeping mud.
Soft as pussywillows sprout,

barncats stretch and kittens bud.
This tidal circle spins me now
and greens my heart at April flood:

the chickadee, the winter sparrow,
blow North to Canada to breed;
a wet snail climbs the new-turned furrow.

A rash of robins land to feed;
pigweed, pokeweed, ragwort, mallow,
spring from summer's drifted seed.

The dogtooth steeps deep yellow
in deep shade. Dandelions sun
the lawn, last week's ponds are shallow.

The knotted grass snake is undone,
and warmer blood expands to know
the vernal course brown conies run.

The year is round around me now:
as I walk, turn, behind the harrow,
my feet take root against tomorrow.

PHILIP BOOTH

Spring Goeth All in White

Spring goeth all in white,
Crowned with milk-white may:
In fleecy flocks of light
O'er heaven the white clouds stray:

White butterflies in the air;
White daisies prank the ground:
The cherry and hoary pear
Scatter their snow around.

ROBERT BRIDGES

Spring

Pleasure it is
   To hear, iwis,*
   The birdës sing.
The deer in the dale,
The sheep in the vale,
   The corn springing;
God's purveyance
For sustenance
   It is for man.
Then we always
To give him praise,
   And thank him than,*
   And thank him than.

WILLIAM CORNISH

* iwis: *indeed;* than: *then*

Talking in Their Sleep

"You think I am dead,"
The apple tree said,
"Because I have never a leaf to show—
Because I stoop
And my branches droop,
And the dull gray mosses over me grow!
But I'm still alive in trunk and shoot;
The buds of next May
I fold away—
But I pity the withered grass at my feet."

"You think I am dead,"
The quick grass said,
"Because I have parted with stem and blade!
But under the ground
I am safe and sound
With the snow's thick blanket over me laid.
I'm all alive and ready to shoot,
Should the spring of the year
Come dancing here—
But I pity the flowers without branch or root."

"You think I am dead,"
A soft voice said,
"Because not a branch or root I own!
I never have died
But close I hide
In a plumy seed that the wind has sown.
Patiently I wait through the long winter hours;
You will see me again—
I shall laugh at you then,
Out of the eyes of a hundred flowers."

EDITH M. THOMAS

Corinna's Going a-Maying

Get up, get up for shame! The blooming morn
Upon her wings presents the god unshorn.
   See how Aurora throws her fair
   Fresh-quilted colors through the air:
   Get up, sweet slug-a-bed, and see
   The dew bespangling herb and tree.
Each flower has wept and bowed toward the east
An hour since; yet you not dressed,
   Nay! not so much as out of bed?
   When all the birds have matins said,
   And sung their thankful hymns: 'tis sin,
   Nay, profanation to keep in,
Whenas a thousand virgins on this day
Spring, sooner than the lark, to fetch in May.

Rise and put on your foliage, and be seen
To come forth, like the springtime, fresh and green,
   And sweet as Flora. Take no care
   For jewels for your gown or hair:
   Fear not, the leaves will strew
   Gems in abundance upon you:
Besides, the childhood of the day has kept,
Against you come, some orient pearls unwept:
   Come and receive them while the light
   Hangs on the dew-locks of the night,
   And Titan on the eastern hill
   Retires himself, or else stands still
Till you come forth. Wash, dress, be brief in praying:
Few beads are best when once we go a-Maying.

Come, my Corinna, come; and coming, mark
How each field turns a street, each street a park
   Made green and trimmed with trees: see how
   Devotion gives each house a bough
   Or branch: each porch, each door, ere this,

An ark, a tabernacle is
Made up of white-thorn neatly interwove;
As if here were those cooler shades of love.
  Can such delights be in the street
  And open fields, and we not see't?
  Come, we'll abroad; and let's obey
  The proclamation made for May,
And sin no more, as we have done, by staying;
But my Corinna, come, let's go a-Maying.

There's not a budding boy or girl this day
But is got up and gone to bring in May.
  A deal of youth, ere this, is come
  Back, and with white-thorn laden home.
  Some have dispatched their cakes and cream
  Before that we have left to dream:
And some have wept and wooed and plighted troth
And chose their priest, ere we can cast off sloth:
  Many a green-gown has been given,
  Many a kiss, both odd and even;
  Many a glance too has been sent
  From out the eye, love's firmament;
Many a jest told of the keys betraying
This night, and locks picked, yet we are not a-Maying.

Come, let us go while we are in our prime,
And take the harmless folly of the time.
  We shall grow old apace, and die
  Before we know our liberty.
  Our life is short, and our days run
  As fast away as does the sun:
And as a vapor, or a drop of rain
Once lost, can ne'er be found again:
  So when or you or I are made
  A fable, song, or fleeting shade,
  All love, all liking, all delight
  Lies drowned with us in endless night.
Then while time serves, and we are but decaying,
Come, my Corinna, come, let's go a-Maying.

ROBERT HERRICK

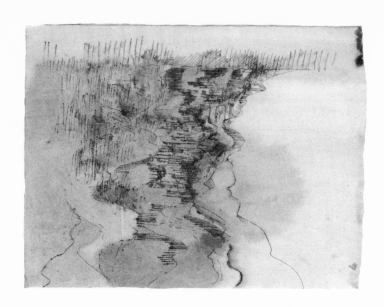

The Enchanted Spring

O'er golden sands my waters flow,
　　With pearls my road is paven white,
Upon my banks sweet flowers blow,
　　And amber rocks direct me right.

Look in my mother-spring; how deep
　　Her dark-green waters, yet how clear!
For joy the pale-eyed stars do weep
　　To see themselves so beauteous here.

Her pebbles all to emeralds turn,
　　Her mosses fine as Nereid's hair,
Bright leaps the crystal from her urn,
　　As pure as dew and twice as rare.

Taste of the wave, 'twill charm thy blood,
　　And make thy cheek outbloom the rose,
'Twill calm thy heart and clear thy mood,
　　Come! sip it freshly as it flows.

GEORGE DARLEY

Beautiful Sunday

It was such a bright morning
That the cows, coming out of the cool dark barns feeling
    a good deal better,
Stood for a while and blinked,
And the young heifers said to each other,
"Oh my!
I never saw such a pretty day!
Let's jump over fences!
Let's go running up and down lanes with our tails in
    the air."
And the old sisterly Jerseys
Thought to themselves, "That patch of white clover
Over in the corner where the woodchucks are
Ought to be about ready for a good going over."

Well, you never saw anything in your life like the way
    the young ducks were acting.
They were tearing in and out of the water
Making enough noise to be heard all over the township;
Even the robins were scandalized
And sat around in the trees looking sideways and one-
    eyed at them.
All the crawdads in that part of the creek
Picked up and moved, and the sober old snake
Slipped off his rock and went for a walk in the briars.

The ghosts of dead spiders
Had been busy all night, and every few feet along the
    road
There was a rope of gossamer.
The old white horse taking two old gray people to
    meeting
Held up his head and said to himself,
"Look at those ropes!
Watch me bust them!
Whammy, there goes another one!

Doggone, I'll bet there isn't another horse in 42 counties
Can run along a road pulling a buggy and busting ropes
    and cables."
And all of a sudden he felt so good
That he threw up his hindquarters and gave a big two-
    legged kick,
And the old gray woman said, "Well, I swan to gracious,"
And the old gray man got all tangled up with the lines
And nearly fell out of the buggy reaching for the whip.
"Whoa, there," he said. "Whoa, there, Roosevelt!
Hold on now! What in the Sam Hill is into you?"

About 14 hundred May apple stems,
With their parasols up, marched down the hill
And all the spring beauties turned up their pale, peaked
    noses
And said, "Don't them May apples
Think they're somebody
With their bumbershoots up!"

Oh, it was a grand day, a specially grand day,
And all the flowers were so sweet
That the butterflies sneezed,
And the young goats and the lambs
Couldn't think of anything special enough
In the way of capers and didos,
So they just stood still and looked wise.

JAKE FALSTAFF

In the Spring

In the Spring a fuller crimson comes upon the robin's
    breast;
In the Spring the wanton lapwing gets himself another
    crest;

In the Spring a livelier iris changes on the burnish'd
    dove;
In the Spring a young man's fancy lightly turns to
    thoughts of love.

ALFRED, LORD TENNYSON

To Blossoms

Fair pledges of a fruitful tree,
    Why do ye fall so fast?
    Your date is not so past;
But you may stay yet here a while,
    To blush and gently smile;
      And go at last.

What, were ye born to be
    An hour or half's delight;
    And so to bid good night?
'Twas pity nature brought ye forth
    Merely to show your worth,
      And lose you quite.

But you are lovely leaves, where we
    May read how soon things have
    Their end, though ne'er so brave:
And after they have shown their pride,
    Like you a while, they glide
      Into the grave.

ROBERT HERRICK

The Spring

When wintry weather's all a-done,
An' brooks do sparkle in the zun,
An' nâisy-builden rooks do vlee
Wi' sticks toward their elem tree;
When birds do zing, an' we can zee
    Upon the boughs the buds o' spring,—
    Then I'm as happy as a king,
        A-vield wi' health an' zunsheen.

Vor then the cowslip's hangèn flower
A-wetted in the zunny shower,
Do grow wi' vi'lets, sweet o' smell,
Bezide the wood-screened graegle's bell;
Where drushes' aggs, wi' sky-blue shell,
    Do lie in mossy nest among
    The thorns, while they do zing their zong
        At evenèn in the zunsheen.

An' God do meäke his win' to blow
An' raïn to vall vor high an' low,
An' bid his mornèn zun to rise
Vor all alike, an' groun' an' skies
Ha' colors vor the poor man's eyes:
    An' in our trials He is near,
    To hear our mwoan an' zee our tear,
        An' turn our clouds to zunsheen.

An' many times when I do vind
Things all goo wrong, an' v'ok unkind,
To zee the happy veedèn herds,
An' hear the zingèn o' the birds,
Do soothe my sorrow mwore than words;
    Vor I do zee that 'tis our sin
    Do meäke woone's soul so dark 'ithin,
        When God would gi'e woone zunsheen.

WILLIAM BARNES

The Anxious Farmer

It was awful long ago
    That I put those seeds around;
And I guess I ought to know
    When I stuck 'em in the ground.
'Cause I noted down the day
    In a little diary book,—
It's gotten losted somewhere and
    I don't know where to look.

But I'm certain anyhow
    They've been planted most a week;
And it must be time by now
    For their little sprouts to peek.
They've been watered every day
    With a very speshul care,
And once or twice I've dug 'em up to
      see if they were there.

I fixed the dirt in humps
    Just the way they said I should;
And I crumbled all the lumps
    Just as finely as I could.
And I found a nangle-worm
    A-poking up his head, —
He maybe feeds on seeds and such,
      and so I squushed him dead.

A seed's so very small,
    And dirt all looks the same; —
How can they know at all
    The way they ought to aim?
And so I'm waiting round
    In case of any need;
A farmer ought to do his best for
      every single seed!

BURGES JOHNSON

Seed Leaves   *To R. F.*

I

Here something stubborn comes,
Dislodging the earth crumbs
And making crusty rubble.
It comes up bending double
And looks like a green staple.
It could be seedling maple,
Or artichoke, or bean;
That remains to be seen.

II

Forced to make choice of ends,
The stalk in time unbends,
Shakes off the seedcase, heaves
Aloft, and spreads two leaves
Which still display no sure
And special signature.
Toothless and fat, they keep
The oval form of sleep.

III

This plant would like to grow
And yet be embryo;
Increase, and yet escape
The doom of taking shape;
Be vaguely vast, and climb
To the tip end of time
With all of space to fill,
Like boundless Yggdrasill
That has the stars for fruit.
But something at the root
More urgent than that urge
Bids two true leaves emerge,

And now the plant, resigned
To being self-defined
Before it can commerce
With the great universe,
Takes aim at all the sky
And starts to ramify.

RICHARD WILBUR

May Day

A delicate fabric of bird song
    Floats in the air,
The smell of wet wild earth
    Is everywhere.

Red small leaves of the maple
    Are clenched like a hand,
Like girls at their first communion
    The pear trees stand.

Oh, I must pass nothing by
    Without loving it much,
The raindrops try with my lips,
    The grass at my touch;

For how can I be sure
    I shall see again
The world on the first of May
    Shining after the rain?

SARA TEASDALE

Memory

My mind lets go a thousand things,
Like dates of wars and deaths of kings,
And yet recalls the very hour—
'Twas noon by yonder village tower,
And on the last blue noon in May—
The wind came briskly up this way,
Crisping the brook beside the road;
Then, pausing here, set down its load
Of pine scents, and shook listlessly
Two petals from that wild-rose tree.

THOMAS BAILEY ALDRICH

Spring Oak

Above the quiet valley and unrippled lake
While woodchucks burrowed new holes, and birds sang,
And radicles began downward and shoots
Committed themselves to the spring
And entered with tiny industrious earthquakes,
A dry-rooted, winter-twisted oak
Revealed itself slowly. And one morning
When the valley underneath was still sleeping
It shook itself and was all green.

GALWAY KINNELL

Green Thoughts in a Green Shade

Flowers and Gardens

from **The Garden**

What wondrous life is this I lead!
Ripe apples drop about my head;
The luscious clusters of the vine
Upon my mouth do crush their wine;
The nectarine, and curious peach,
Into my hands themselves do reach;
Stumbling on melons, as I pass,
Insnared with flowers, I fall on grass.

Meanwhile the mind, from pleasure less,
Withdraws into its happiness;
The mind, that ocean where each kind
Does straight its own resemblance find;
Yet it creates, transcending these,
Far other worlds, and other seas,
Annihilating all that's made
To a green thought in a green shade.

Here at the fountain's sliding foot,
Or at some fruit tree's mossy root,
Casting the body's vest aside,
My soul into the boughs does glide;
There, like a bird, it sits and sings,
Then wets and combs its silver wings,
And, till prepared for longer flight,
Waves in its plumes the various light.

ANDREW MARVELL

A Contemplation upon Flowers

Brave flowers, that I could gallant it like you
    And be as little vain!
You come abroad, and make a harmless show,
    And to your beds of earth again;
You are not proud, you know your birth,
For your embroidered garments are from earth.

You do obey your months, and times, but I
    Would have it ever spring;
My fate would know no winter, never die,
    Nor think of such a thing.
Oh that I could my bed of earth but view,
And smile, and look as cheerfully as you!

Oh teach me to see death, and not to fear,
    But rather to take truce;
How often have I seen you at a bier,
    And there look fresh and spruce.
You fragrant flowers then teach me that my breath
Like yours may sweeten and perfume my death.

HENRY KING

The Gardener

The gardener in his old brown hands
Turns over the brown earth,
As if he loves and understands
The flowers before their birth,
The fragile little childish strands
He buries in the earth.

Like pious children one by one
He sets them head by head,
And draws the clothes, when all is done,
Closely about each head,
And leaves his children to sleep on
In the one quiet bed.

ARTHUR SYMONS

The Idle Flowers

I have sown upon the fields
Eyebright and Pimpernel,
And Pansy and Poppy-seed
Ripen'd and scatter'd well,

And silver Lady-smock
The meads with light to fill,
Cowslip and Buttercup,
Daisy and Daffodil;

King-cup and Fleur-de-lys
Upon the marsh to meet
With Comfrey, Watermint,
Loose-strife and Meadowsweet;

And all along the stream
My care hath not forgot
Crowfoot's white galaxy
And love's Forget-me-not:

And where high grasses wave
Shall great Moon-daisies blink,
With Rattle and Sorrel sharp
And Robin's ragged pink.

Thick on the woodland floor
Gay company shall be,
Primrose and Hyacinth
And frail Anemone,

Perennial Strawberry-bloom,
Woodsorrel's penciled veil,
Dishevel'd Willow-weed
And Orchis purple and pale,

Bugle, that blushes blue,
And Woodruff's snowy gem,
Proud Foxglove's finger-bells
And Spurge with milky stem.

High on the downs so bare,
Where thou dost love to climb,
Pink Thrift and Milkwort are,
Lotus and scented Thyme;

And in the shady lanes
Bold Arum's hood of green,
Herb Robert, Violet,
Starwort and Celandine;

And by the dusty road
Bedstraw and Mullein tall,
With red Valerian
And Toadflax on the wall,

Yarrow and Chicory,
That hath for hue no like,
Silene and Mallow mild
And Agrimony's spike,

Blue-eyed Veronicas
And gray-faced Scabious
And downy Silverweed
And striped Convolvulus:

Harebell shall haunt the banks,
And thro' the hedgerow peer
Withwind and Snapdragon
And Nightshade's flower of fear.

And where men never sow,
Have I my Thistles set,
Ragwort and stiff Wormwood
And straggling Mignonette,

Bugloss and Burdock rank
And prickly Teasel high,
With Umbels yellow and white,
That come to kexes dry.

Pale Chlora shalt thou find,
Sun-loving Centaury,
Cranesbill and Sinjunwort,
Cinquefoil and Betony:

Shock-headed Dandelion,
That drank the fire of the sun:
Hawkweed and Marigold,
Cornflower and Campion.

Let Oak and Ash grow strong,
Let Beech her branches spread;
Let Grass and Barley throng
And waving Wheat for bread;

Be share and sickle bright
To labor at all hours;
For thee and thy delight
I have made the idle flowers.

But now 'tis Winter, child,
And bitter northwinds blow,
The ways are wet and wild,
The land is laid in snow.

ROBERT BRIDGES

The Round

Skunk cabbage, bloodroot,
ginseng, spring beauty,
Dutchman's-breeches,
rue, and betony;

bluets, columbine,
cowslip and bittercress,
heartleaf, anemone,
lupin, arbutus;

bunchberry, merrybells,
Jack-in-the-pulpit,
hepatica, vetch,
and dogtooth violet;

pussy-willow, starwort,
wet-dog trillium,
alumroot, lady's-slipper,
Solomon's-plume;

milkweed, fireweed,
loosestrife and dogbane,
sunbright, buttercup,
thistle, and pipevine;

paintbrush, bunchlily,
chicory, candy-root,
spatterdock, sundew,
touch-me-not;

goldenrod, aster,
burdock and coral-
root, gentian, ragweed,
jumpseed, and sorrel;

upland yellow-eye
and Joe-pye-weed,
bittersweet, sumac,
snow, and frozen seed.

PHILIP BOOTH

A Garden Song

I have a garden of my own,
    Shining with flowers of every hue;
I love it dearly while alone,
    But I shall love it more with you:
And there the golden bees shall crone,
    In summertime at break of morn,
And wake us with their busy hum
    Around the Siha's fragrant thorn.

I have a fawn from Aden's land,
    On leafy buds and berries nurst;
And you shall feed him from your hand,
    Though he may start with fear at first.
And I will lead you where he lies
    For shelter in the noon-tide heat;
And you may touch his sleepy eyes,
    And feel his little silvery feet.

THOMAS MOORE

Flower in the Crannied Wall

Flower in the crannied wall,
I pluck you out of the crannies,
I hold you here, root and all, in my hand,
Little flower—but if I could understand
What you are, root and all, and all in all,
I should know what God and man is.

ALFRED, LORD TENNYSON

The Big Nasturtiums

All of a sudden the big nasturtiums
Rose in the night from the ocean's bed,
Rested a while in the light of the morning,
Turning the sand dunes tiger red.

They covered the statue of Abraham Lincoln,
They climbed to the top of our church's spire.
"Grandpa! Grandpa! Come to the window!
Come to the window! Our world's on fire!"

Big nasturtiums in the High Sierras,
Big nasturtiums in the lands below;
Our trains are late and our planes have fallen,
And out in the ocean the whistles blow.

Over the fields and over the forests,
Over the living and over the dead—
"I never expected the big nasturtiums
To come in my lifetime!" Grandpa said.

ROBERT BEVERLY HALE

from A Midsummer Night's Dream

I know a bank whereon the wild thyme blows,
Where ox-lips and the nodding violet grows;
Quite overcanopied with lush woodbine,
With sweet musk roses, and with eglantine:
There sleeps Titania some time of the night,
Lull'd in these flowers with dances and delight;
And there the snake throws her enamell'd skin,
Weed wide enough to wrap a fairy in.

WILLIAM SHAKESPEARE

The Indolent Gardener

Jungle
>   takes over the garden.
Day after day creepers weave impenetrable walls.
Flowers have gone wild, making a woven defense against
>   intruders,
their strong roots intertwined, to trip, to overthrow.
The jewel weed grows tall and thick.
Great branches lie where they have fallen,
the tree uprooted, blocking the paths, blotting out the
>   sky.
On sunniest days scars of hurricane are on this land.

Some morning
>   monkeys will come trooping and chattering.
Tigers will slink through the forest of phlox,
rutile deer romp and leap through the mock orange,
panthers drop from the tree limbs that grasp and tangle
>   over the pool:
from quince and pear and wild willow, out of grape
>   leaves grasping the top of the elm,
black panthers will drop.
Elephants will push through the sagging pergola,
a bird of paradise alight on the blighted maple,
while peach-colored parakeets sit in innocent pairs
on the stone wall among the euonymous.
When night falls, mouse-like nocturnal creatures will slip
>   out of the heaving ground
to scamper in the moonlight.

Then
>   will the bulbul sing its enchanting song . . .
Until I forget vanished larkspur and madonna lilies,
and the civilized scent of herbs.

MARY KENNEDY

My Garden

The lilac in my garden comes to bloom,
    The apple, plum and cherry wait their hour,
The honeysuckle climbs from pole to pole—
    And the rockery has a stone that's now a flower,
Jeweled by moss in every tiny hole!

Close to my lilac there's a small bird's nest
    Of quiet, young, half-sleeping birds: but when
I look, each little rascal—five I've reckoned—
    Opens a mouth so large and greedy then,
He swallows his own face in half a second!

W. H. DAVIES

A Garden Song

Here in this sequestered close
Bloom the hyacinth and rose,
Here beside the modest stock
Flaunts the flaring hollyhock;
Here, without a pang, one sees
Ranks, conditions and degrees.

All the seasons run their race
In this quiet resting place;
Peach and apricot and fig
Here will ripen and grow big;
Here is store and overplus,—
More had not Alcinoüs!

Here, in alleys cool and green,
Far ahead the thrush is seen;
Here along the southern wall
Keeps the bee his festival;
All is quiet else—afar
Sounds of toil and turmoil are.

Here be shadows large and long;
Here be spaces meet for song;
Grant, O garden-god, that I,
Now that none profane is nigh,—
Now that mood and moment please,—
Find the fair Pierides!

AUSTIN DOBSON

'Tis the Last Rose of Summer

'Tis the last rose of summer,
    Left blooming alone;
All her lovely companions
    Are faded and gone;
No flower of her kindred,
    No rosebud is nigh,
To reflect back her blushes,
    Or give sigh for sigh.

I'll not leave thee, thou lone one!
    To pine on the stem;
Since the lovely are sleeping,
    Go, sleep thou with them.
Thus kindly I scatter
    Thy leaves o'er the bed
Where thy mates of the garden
    Lie scentless and dead.

So soon may *I* follow,
    When friendships decay,
And from Love's shining circle
    The gems drop away.
When true hearts lie withered,
    And fond ones are flown,
O who would inhabit
    This bleak world alone?

THOMAS MOORE

A Cut Flower

I stand on slenderness all fresh and fair,
I feel root-firmness in the earth far down,
I catch in the wind and loose my scent for bees
That sack my throat for kisses and suck love.
What is the wind that brings thy body over?
Wind, I am beautiful and sick. I long
For rain that strikes and bites like cold and hurts.
Be angry, rain, for dew is kind to me
When I am cool from sleep and take my bath.

Who softens the sweet earth about my feet,
Touches my face so often and brings water?
Where does she go, taller than any sunflower
Over the grass like birds? Has she a root?
These are great animals that kneel to us,
Sent by the sun perhaps to help us grow.
I have seen death. The colors went away,
The petals grasped at nothing and curled tight.
Then the whole head fell off and left the sky.

She tended me and held me by my stalk.
Yesterday I was well, and then the gleam,
The thing sharper than frost cut me in half.
I fainted and was lifted high. I feel
Waist-deep in rain. My face is dry and drawn.
My beauty leaks into the glass like rain.
When first I opened to the sun I thought
My colors would be parched. Where are my bees?
Must I die now? Is this a part of life?

KARL SHAPIRO

To Daffodils

Fair daffodils, we weep to see
        You haste away so soon:
As yet the early-rising sun
        Has not attained his noon.
                        Stay, stay,
                Until the hasting day
                        Has run
                But to the evensong;
And, having prayed together, we
                Will go with you along.

We have short time to stay, as you,
        We have as short a spring;
As quick a growth to meet decay,
        As you, or anything.
                        We die,
                As your hours do, and dry
                        Away,
                Like to the summer's rain;
Or as the pearls of morning's dew
                Ne'er to be found again.

ROBERT HERRICK

I Wandered Lonely as a Cloud

I wandered lonely as a cloud
That floats on high o'er vales and hills,
When all at once I saw a crowd,
A host, of golden daffodils;
Beside the lake, beneath the trees,
Fluttering and dancing in the breeze.

Continuous as the stars that shine
And twinkle in the milky way,
They stretched in never-ending line
Along the margin of a bay:
Ten thousand saw I at a glance,
Tossing their heads in sprightly dance.

The waves beside them danced; but they
Outdid the sparkling waves in glee:
A poet could not be gay,
In such a jocund company:
I gazed—and gazed—but little thought
What wealth the show to me had brought:

For oft, when on my couch I lie,
In vacant or in pensive mood,
They flash upon that inward eye
Which is the bliss of solitude;
And then my heart with pleasure fills,
And dances with the daffodils.

WILLIAM WORDSWORTH

The Daisy

Wee, modest, crimson-tipped flow'r,
Thou'st met me in an evil hour;
For I maun* crush amang the stoure*
    Thy slender stem:
To spare thee now is past my pow'r,
    Thou bonie gem.

Alas! it's no' thy neebor sweet,
The bonie lark, companion meet,
Bending thee 'mang the dewy weet,
    Wi' spreckl'd breast!
When, upward-springing, blythe, to greet
    The purpling east.

Cauld blew the bitter-biting north
Upon thy early, humble birth;
Yet cheerfully thou glinted forth
    Amid the storm,
Scarce rear'd above the parent-earth
    Thy tender form.

The flaunting flow'rs our gardens yield,
High sheltering woods and wa's maun shield:
But thou, beneath the random bield*
    O' clod or stane,
Adorns the histic stibble-field,
    Unseen, alone.

There, in thy scanty mantle clad,
Thy snawie* bosom sun-ward spread,
Thou lifts thy unassuming head
    In humble guise:
But now the share uptears thy bed,
    And low thou lies!

ROBERT BURNS

* maun: *must;* stoure: *strong;* bield: *shield;* snawie: *snowy*

The Daisies

Over the shoulders and slopes of the dune
I saw the white daisies go down to the sea,
A host in the sunshine, an army in June,
The people God sends us to set our heart free.

The bobolinks rallied them up from the dell,
The orioles whistled them out of the wood;
And all of their saying was, "Earth, it is well!"
And all of their dancing was, "Life, thou art good!"

BLISS CARMAN

Daisy's Song

I

The sun, with his great eye,
Sees not so much as I;
And the moon, all silver-proud,
Might as well be in a cloud.

II

And O the spring—the spring
I lead the life of a king!
Couch'd in the teeming grass,
I spy each pretty lass.

III

I look where no one dares,
And I stare where no one stares,
And when the night is nigh,
Lambs bleat my lullaby.

JOHN KEATS

The Rhodora:

On Being Asked,
Whence Is the Flower?

In May, when sea winds pierced our solitudes,
I found the fresh Rhodora in the woods,
Spreading its leafless blooms in a damp nook,
To please the desert and the sluggish brook.
The purple petals, fallen in the pool,
Made the black water with their beauty gay;
Here might the redbird come his plumes to cool,
And court the flower that cheapens his array.
Rhodora! if the sages ask thee why
This charm is wasted on the earth and sky,
Tell them, dear, that if eyes were made for seeing,
Then Beauty is its own excuse for being:
Why thou wert there, O rival of the rose!
I never thought to ask, I never knew:
But, in my simple ignorance, suppose
The selfsame Power that brought me there brought you.

RALPH WALDO EMERSON

Irises

Where are they now, the softly blooming flowers
With name unhard, unbarred, the Irises?
Their stalks are shears stuck in the hardened ground.
We named their colors, but our sights could measure
Never their colors' depths. Where are they now
With argent, purple, azure and pale gold,
And colors doubled like two stains in glass—
Light-plumed Irises, where are they now?

PADRAIC COLUM

Sunflower

Sunflower, of flowers
the most lonely,
yardstick of hours,
long-term stander
in empty spaces,
shunner of bowers,
indolent bender
seldom, in only
the sharpest of showers:
tell us, why
is it your face is
a snarl of jet swirls
and gold arrows, a burning
old lion face high
in a cornflower sky,
yet by turning
your head, we find
you wear a girl's
bonnet behind?

JOHN UPDIKE

Of Neptune's Empire
Let Us Sing

Rivers, Lakes, and the Sea

In Praise of Neptune

Of Neptune's empire let us sing,
At whose command the waves obey;
To whom the rivers tribute pay,
Down the high mountains sliding;
To whom the scaly nation yields
Homage for the crystal fields
    Wherein they dwell;
And every sea god pays a gem
Yearly out of his watery cell,
To deck great Neptune's diadem.

The Tritons dancing in a ring,
Before his palace gates do make
The water with their echoes quake,
Like the great thunder sounding:
The sea nymphs chant their accents shrill,
And the Sirens taught to kill
    With their sweet voice,
Make every echoing rock reply,
Unto their gentle murmuring noise,
The praise of Neptune's empery.

THOMAS CAMPION

The Brook

I come from haunts of coot and hern,
    I make a sudden sally,
And sparkle out among the fern,
    To bicker down a valley.

By thirty hills I hurry down,
    Or slip between the ridges,
By twenty thorps, a little town,
    And half a hundred bridges.

Till last by Philip's farm I flow
    To join the brimming river,
For men may come and men may go
    But I go on for ever.

I chatter over stony ways,
    In little sharps and trebles,
I bubble into eddying bays,
    I babble on the pebbles.

With many a curve my banks I fret
    By many a field and fallow,
And many a fairy foreland set
    With willow-weed and mallow.

I chatter, chatter, as I flow
    To join the brimming river,
For men may come and men may go,
    But I go on for ever.

I wind about, and in and out,
    With here a blossom sailing,
And here and there a lusty trout,
    And here and there a grayling,

And here and there a foamy flake
    Upon me, as I travel
With many a silvery waterbreak
    Above the golden gravel,

And draw them all along, and flow
    To join the brimming river,
For men may come and men may go,
    But I go on for ever.

I steal by lawns and grassy plots,
    I slide by hazel covers;
I move the sweet forget-me-nots
    That grow for happy lovers.

I slip, I slide, I gloom, I glance,
    Among my skimming swallows;
I make the netted sunbeam dance
    Against my sandy shallows.

I murmur under moon and stars
    In brambly wildernesses;
I linger by my shingly bars;
    I loiter round my cresses;

And out again I curve and flow
    To join the brimming river,
For men may come and men may go,
    But I go on for ever.

ALFRED, LORD TENNYSON

The Hurrying Brook

With half a hundred sudden loops and coils
Between the limits of two humble farms,
Swerving and dodging like a boy who foils
His mates' pursuit; with numberless wild charms;
With beauty and joy my tiny river dances
The longest way he can, and prettiest too,
About our meadows, topped with shining lances
Of reed and rush, tunneled in shadowy blue
Of thicket oak and alder and ivied shell
Of vast old willow; fast he runs and well
To keep his many appointments all at once,
Now the eel-stone, now the yellow lily, now the white,
Now where the fat vole on the clay ledge suns,
Here there and everywhere, a brilliant watersprite.

EDMUND BLUNDEN

Hyla Brook

By June our brook's run out of song and speed.
Sought for much after that, it will be found
Either to have gone groping underground
(And taken with it all the Hyla breed *
That shouted in the mist a month ago,
Like ghost of sleigh-bells in a ghost of snow)—
Or flourished and come up in jewel-weed,
Weak foliage that is blown upon and bent
Even against the way its waters went.
Its bed is left a faded paper sheet
Of dead leaves stuck together by the heat—
A brook to none but who remember long.
This as it will be seen is other far
Than with brooks taken otherwhere in song.
We love the things we love for what they are.

ROBERT FROST

* Hyla breed: *frogs*

Lives

You cannot cage a field.
You cannot wire it, as you wire a summer's roses
To sell in towns; you cannot cage it
Or kill it utterly. All you can do is to force
Year after year from the stream to the cold woods
The heavy glitter of wheat, till its body tires
And the yield grows weaker and dies. But the field never dies,
Though you build on it, burn it black, or domicile
A thousand prisoners upon its empty features.
You cannot kill a field. A field will reach
Right under the streams to touch the limbs of its brothers.

But you can cage the woods.
You can throw up fences, as round a recalcitrant heart
Spring up remonstrances. You can always cage the woods,
Hold them completely. Confine them to hill or valley,
You can alter their face, their shape; uprooting their outer saplings
You can even alter their wants, and their smallest longings
Press to your own desires. The woods succumb
To the paths made through their life, withdraw the trees,
Betake themselves where you tell them, and acquiesce.
The woods retreat; their protest of leaves whirls
Pitifully to the cooling heavens, like dead or dying prayers.

But what can you do with a stream?
You can widen it here, or deepen it there, but even
If you alter its course entirely it gives the impression
That this is what it always wanted. Moorhens return
To nest or hide in the reeds which quickly grow up there,
The fishes breed in it, stone settles on to stone.
The stream announces its places where the water will bubble
Daily and unconcerned, contentedly ruffling and scuffling
With the drifting sky or the leaf. Whatever you do,
A stream has rights, for a stream is always water;
To cross it you have to bridge it, and it will not flow uphill.

HENRY REED

Water Noises

When I am playing by myself,
    And all the boys are lost around,
Then I can hear the water go—
    It makes a little talking sound.

Along the rocks below the tree,
    I see it ripple up and wink;
And I can hear it saying on,
    "And do you think? and do you think?"

A bug shoots by that snaps and ticks,
    And a bird flies up beside the tree
To go into the sky to sing.
    I hear it say, "Killdee, killdee!"

Or else a yellow cow comes down
    To splash a while and have a drink.
But when she goes I still can hear
    The water say, "And do you think?"

ELIZABETH MADOX ROBERTS

The Brook in February

A snowy path for squirrel and fox,
    It winds between the wintry firs.
Snow-muffled are its iron rocks,
    And o'er its stillness nothing stirs.

But low, bend low a listening ear!
    Beneath the mask of moveless white
A babbling whisper you shall hear
    Of birds and blossoms, leaves and light.

CHARLES G. D. ROBERTS

from The Bothie of Tober-na-Vuolich

There is a stream, I name not its name, lest inquisitive
tourist
Hunt it, and make it a lion, and get it at last into guide
books,
Springing far off from a loch unexplored in the folds of
great mountains,
Falling two miles through rowan and stunted alder,
enveloped
Then for four more in a forest of pine, where broad and ample
Spreads, to convey it, the glen with heathery slopes on
both sides:
Broad and fair the stream, with occasional falls and narrows;
But, where the glen of its course approaches the vale of
the river,
Met and blocked by a huge interposing mass of granite,
Scarce by a channel deep-cut, raging up, and raging onward,
Forces its flood through a passage so narrow a lady would
step it.
There, across the great rocky wharves, a wooden bridge
goes,
Carrying a path to the forest; below, three hundred yards, say,
Lower in level some twenty-five feet, through flats of
shingle,
Stepping stones and a cart track cross in the open valley.
But in the interval here the boiling, pent-up water
Frees itself by a final descent, attaining a bason,
Ten feet wide and eighteen long, with whiteness and fury
Occupied partly, but mostly pellucid, pure, a mirror;
Beautiful there for the color derived from green rocks
under;
Beautiful, most of all, where beads of foam uprising
Mingle their clouds of white with the delicate hue of the
stillness.
Cliff over cliff for its sides, with rowan and pendant birch
boughs,

Here it lies, unthought of above at the bridge and pathway,
Still more enclosed from below by wood and rocky
      projection.
You are shut in, left alone with yourself and perfection
      of water,
Hid on all sides, left alone with yourself and the goddess
      of bathing.
    Here, the pride of the plunger, you stride the fall and
      clear it;
Here the delight of the bather, you roll in beaded
      sparklings,
Here into pure green depth drop down from lofty ledges.

ARTHUR HUGH CLOUGH

Song of the Chattahoochee

    Out of the hills of Habersham,
    Down the valleys of Hall,
I hurry amain to reach the plain,
Run the rapid and leap the fall,
Split at the rock and together again,
Accept my bed, or narrow or wide,
And flee from folly on every side
With a lover's pain to attain the plain
    Far from the hills of Habersham,
    Far from the valleys of Hall.

    All down the hills of Habersham,
    All through the valleys of Hall,
The rushes cried *Abide, abide,*
The willful waterweeds held me thrall,
The laving laurel turned my tide.
The ferns and the fondling grass said *Stay,*
The dewberry dipped for to work delay,
And the little reeds sighed *Abide, abide,*
    Here in the hills of Habersham,
    Here in the valleys of Hall.

High o'er the hills of Habersham,
　　Veiling the valleys of Hall,
The hickory told me manifold
Fair tales of shade, the poplar tall
Wrought me her shadowy self to hold,
The chestnut, the oak, the walnut, the pine,
Overleaning, with flickering meaning and sign,
Said, *Pass not, so cold, these manifold*
　　Deep shades of the hills of Habersham,
　　These glades in the valleys of Hall.

And oft in the hills of Habersham,
　　And oft in the valleys of Hall,
The white quartz shone, and the smooth brook stone
Did bar me of passage with friendly brawl,
And many a luminous jewel lone
—Crystals clear or a-cloud with mist,
Ruby, garnet, and amethyst—
Made lures with the lights of streaming stone
　　In the clefts of the hills of Habersham,
　　In the beds of the valleys of Hall.

But oh, not the hills of Habersham,
　　And oh, not the valleys of Hall
Avail: I am fain for to water the plain.
Downward the voices of Duty call—
Downward, to toil and be mixed with the main,
The dry fields burn, and the mills are to turn,
And a myriad flowers mortally yearn,
And the lordly main from beyond the plain
　　Calls o'er the hills of Habersham,
　　Calls through the valleys of Hall.

SIDNEY LANIER

The Gravedigger

Oh, the shambling sea is a sexton old,
And well his work is done.
With an equal grave for lord and knave,
He buries them every one.

Then hoy and rip, with a rolling hip,
He makes for the nearest shore;
And God, who sent him a thousand ship,
Will send him a thousand more;

But some he'll save for a bleaching grave,
And shoulder them in to shore,—
Shoulder them in, shoulder them in,
Shoulder them in to shore.

Oh, the ships of Greece and the ships of Tyre
Went out, and where are they?
In the port they made, they are delayed
With the ships of yesterday.

He followed the ships of England far,
As the ships of long ago;
And the ships of France they led him a dance,
But he laid them all arow.

Oh, a loafing, idle lubber to him
Is the sexton of the town;
For sure and swift, with a guiding lift,
He shovels the dead men down;

But though he delves so fierce and grim,
His honest graves are wide,
But some he'll save for a bleaching grave,
And shoulder them in to shore,—
Shoulder them in, shoulder them in,
Shoulder them in to shore.

BLISS CARMAN

Afton Water

Flow gently, sweet Afton, among thy green braes;
Flow gently, I'll sing thee a song in thy praise;
My Mary's asleep by thy murmuring stream,
Flow gently, sweet Afton, disturb not her dream.

Thou stock dove whose echo resounds through the glen,
Ye wild whistling blackbirds in yon thorny den,
Thou green-crested lapwing, thy screaming forbear;
I charge you disturb not my slumbering fair.

How lofty, sweet Afton, thy neighboring hills,
Far marked with the courses of clear-winding rills!
There daily I wander as noon rises high,
My flocks and my Mary's sweet cot in my eye.

How pleasant thy banks and green valleys below,
Where wild in the woodlands the primroses blow!
There oft as mild evening weeps over the lea,
The sweet-scented birk shades my Mary and me.

Thy crystal stream, Afton, how lovely it glides,
And winds by the cot where my Mary resides;
How wanton thy waters her snowy feet lave,
As, gathering sweet flowerets, she stems thy clear wave!

Flow gently, sweet Afton, among thy green braes;
Flow gently, sweet river, the theme of my lays;
My Mary's asleep by thy murmuring stream,
Flow gently, sweet Afton, disturb not her dream.

ROBERT BURNS

The Tide River

Clear and cool, clear and cool,
By laughing shallow, and dreaming pool;
Cool and clear, cool and clear,
By shining shingle, and foaming wear;
Under the crag where the ouzel sings,
And the ivied wall where the church bell rings,
Undefiled, for the undefiled;
Play by me, bathe in me, mother and child.

Dank and foul, dank and foul,
By the smoky town in its murky cowl:
Foul and dank, foul and dank,
By wharf and sewer and slimy bank;
Darker and darker the further I go,
Baser and baser the richer I grow;
Who dare sport with the sin-defiled?
Shrink from me, turn from me, mother and child.

Strong and free, strong and free,
The floodgates are open, away to the sea.
Free and strong, free and strong,
Cleansing my streams as I hurry along
To the golden sands, and the leaping bar,
And the taintless tide that awaits me afar,
As I lose myself in the infinite main,
Like a soul that has sinned and is pardoned again.
Undefiled, for the undefiled;
Play by me, bathe in me, mother and child.

CHARLES KINGSLEY

By the Sea

Why does the sea moan evermore?
    Shut out from heaven it makes its moan,
It frets against the boundary shore;
    All earth's full rivers cannot fill
    The sea, that drinking thirsteth still.

Sheer miracles of loveliness
    Lie hid in its unlooked-on bed:
Anemones, salt, passionless,
    Blow flower-like; just enough alive
    To blow and multiply and thrive.

Shells quaint with curve, or spot, or spike,
    Encrusted live things argus-eyed,
All fair alike, yet all unlike,
    Are born without a pang, and die
    Without a pang, and so pass by.

CHRISTINA ROSSETTI

Tweed and Till

Says Tweed to Till*—
    "What gars ye rin sae still?"
Says Till to Tweed—
"Though ye rin with speed
    And I rin slaw,
For ae man that ye droon
    I droon twa."

ANONYMOUS

* Tweed and Till: *Rivers of Scotland and Northern England*

The Sea

You, you are all unloving, loveless, you;
Restless and lonely, shaken by your own moods,
You are celibate and single, scorning a comrade even,
Threshing your own passions with no woman for the
    threshing floor,
Finishing your dreams for your own sake only,
Playing your great game around the world, alone,
Without playmate, or helpmate, having no one to cherish,
No one to comfort, and refusing any comforter.

Not like the earth, the spouse all full of increase
Moiled over with the rearing of her many-mouthed
    young;
You are single, you are fruitless, phosphorescent, cold and
    callous,
Naked of worship, of love or of adornment,
Scorning the panacea even of labor,
Sworn to a high and splendid purposelessness
Of brooding and delighting in the secret of life's goings,
Sea, only you are free, sophisticated.

You who toil not, you who spin not,
Surely but for you and your like, toiling
Were not worth while, nor spinning worth the effort!

You who take the moon as in a sieve, and sift
Her flake by flake and spread her meaning out;
You who roll the stars like jewels in your palm,
So that they seem to utter themselves aloud;
You who steep from out the days their color,
Reveal the universal tint that dyes
Their web; who shadow the sun's great gestures and
    expressions
So that he seems a stranger in his passing;

Who voice the dumb night fittingly;
Sea, you shadow of all things, now mock us to death with
    your shadowing.

D. H. LAWRENCE

The World Below the Brine

The world below the brine;
Forests at the bottom of the sea—the branches and leaves,
Sea lettuce, vast lichens, strange flowers and seeds—the
    thick tangle, the openings, and the pink turf,
Different colors, pale gray and green, purple, white, and
    gold—the play of light through the water,
Dumb swimmers there among the rocks—coral, gluten,
    grass, rushes—and the aliment of the swimmers,
Sluggish existences grazing there, suspended, or slowly
    crawling close to the bottom,
The sperm whale at the surface, blowing air and spray,
    or disporting with his flukes,
The leaden-eyed shark, the walrus, the turtle, the hairy
    sea leopard, and the sting ray;
Passions there—wars, pursuits, tribes—sight in those ocean
    depths—breathing that thick-breathing air, as so many
    do;
The change thence to the sight here, and to the subtle
    air breathed by beings like us, who walk this sphere;
The change onward from ours, to that of beings who
    walk other spheres.

WALT WHITMAN

Fragment

The cataract, whirling to the precipice,
    Elbows down rocks and, shouldering, thunders
        through.
Roars, howls, and stifled murmurs never cease;
    Hell and its agonies seem hid below.
Thick rolls the mist, that smokes and falls in dew;
    The trees and greenwood wear the deepest green.
Horrible mysteries in the gulf stare through,
    Roars of a million tongues, and none knows what
        they mean.

JOHN CLARE

Sea Lullaby

The old moon is tarnished
With smoke of the flood,
The dead leaves are varnished
With color like blood,

A treacherous smiler
With teeth white as milk,
A savage beguiler
In sheathings of silk,

The sea creeps to pillage,
She leaps on her prey;
A child of the village
Was murdered today.

She came up to greet him
In a smooth golden cloak,
She choked him and beat him
To death, for a joke.

Her bright locks were tangled,
She shouted for joy,
With one hand she strangled
A strong little boy.

Now in silence she lingers
Beside him all night
To wash her long fingers
In silvery light.

ELINOR WYLIE

Afternoon: Amagansett Beach

          The broad beach,
Sea wind and the sea's irregular rhythm,
Great dunes with their pale grass, and on the beach
Driftwood, tangle of bones, an occasional shell,
Now coarse, now carven and delicate—whorls of time
Stranded in space, deaf ears listening
To lost time, old oceanic secrets.
Along the water's edge, in pattern casual
As the pattern of the stars, the pin-point air holes
Left by the sand flea under the receding spume,
Wink and blink out again. A gull drifts over,
Wide wings crucified against the sky—
His shadow travels the shore; upon its margins
You will find his signature: one long line,
Two shorter lines curving out from it, a nearly
Perfect graph of the bird himself in flight.
His footprint is his image fallen from heaven.

JOHN HALL WHEELOCK

Sea-weed

Sea-weed sways and sways and swirls
as if swaying were its form of stillness;
and if it flushes against fierce rock
it slips over it as shadows do, without hurting itself.

D. H. LAWRENCE

O Billows Bounding Far

O billows bounding far,
How wet, how wet ye are!

When first my gaze ye met
I said "Those waves are wet."

I said it, and am quite
Convinced that I was right.

Who saith that ye are dry?
I give that man the lie.

Thy wetness, O thou sea,
Is wonderful to me.

It agitates my heart,
To think how wet thou art.

No object I have met
Is more profoundly wet.

Methinks 'twere vain to try,
O sea, to wipe thee dry.

I therefore will refrain.
Farewell, thou humid main.

A. E. HOUSMAN

Here, In This Little Bay

Here, in this little Bay,
Full of tumultuous life and great repose,
Where, twice a day,
The purposeless, glad ocean comes and goes,
Under high cliffs, and far from the huge town,
I sit me down.
For want of me the world's course will not fail:
When all its work is done, the lie shall rot;
The truth is great, and shall prevail,
When none cares whether it prevail or not.

COVENTRY PATMORE

Spray

It is a wonder foam is so beautiful.
A wave bursts in anger on a rock, broken up
in a wild white sibilant spray
and falls back, drawing in its breath with rage,
with frustration how beautiful!

D. H. LAWRENCE

Lobster Cove Shindig

If there's a wind, we get it
Straight from the shoulder of rock,
Bowling over boulders
Racketing through the house
Spray steaming mists rolling
Daisies ducking in the hullabaloo.
What a brawl   until the sun appears
Majestic, like the law.

LILLIAN MORRISON

The Cliff-top

The cliff-top has a carpet
    Of lilac, gold and green:
The blue sky bounds the ocean,
    The white clouds scud between.

A flock of gulls are wheeling
    And wailing round my seat;
Above my head the heaven,
    The sea beneath my feet.

ROBERT BRIDGES

The Shell

I

And then I pressed the shell
Close to my ear,
And listened well.

And straightway, like a bell,
Came low and clear
The slow, sad, murmur of far distant seas

Whipped by an icy breeze
Upon a shore
Wind-swept and desolate.

It was a sunless strand that never bore
The footprint of a man.
Nor felt the weight

Since time began
Of any human quality or stir,
Save what the dreary winds and wave incur.

II

And in the hush of waters was the sound
Of pebbles, rolling round;
For ever rolling, with a hollow sound:

And bubbling sea-weeds, as the waters go,
Swish to and fro
Their long cold tentacles of slimy gray:

There was no day;
Nor ever came a night
Setting the stars alight

To wonder at the moon:
Was twilight only, and the frightened croon,
Smitten to whimpers, of the dreary wind

And waves that journeyed blind . . .
And then I loosed my ear—Oh, it was sweet
To hear a cart go jolting down the street.

JAMES STEPHENS

from **Maud**

See what a lovely shell,
Small and pure as a pearl,
Lying close to my foot,
Frail, but a work divine,
Made so fairily well
With delicate spire and whorl,
How exquisitely minute,
A miracle of design!

What is it? a learned man
Could give it a clumsy name.
Let him name it who can,
The beauty would be the same.

The tiny cell is forlorn,
Void of the little living will
That made it stir on the shore.
Did he stand at the diamond door
Of his house in a rainbow frill?
Did he push, when he was uncurl'd,
A golden foot or a fairy horn
Thro' his dim water-world?

Slight, to be crush'd with a tap
Of my fingernail on the sand,
Small, but a work divine,
Frail, but of force to withstand,
Year upon year, the shock
Of cataract seas that snap
The three decker's oaken spine
Athwart the ledges of rock,
Here on the Breton strand!

ALFRED, LORD TENNYSON

Water Picture

In the pond in the park
all things are doubled:
Long buildings hang and
wriggle gently. Chimneys
are bent legs bouncing
on clouds below. A flag
wags like a fishhook
down there in the sky.

The arched stone bridge
is an eye, with underlid
in the water. In its lens
dip crinkled heads with hats
that don't fall off. Dogs go by,
barking on their backs.
A baby, taken to feed the
ducks, dangles upside down,
a pink balloon for a buoy.

Treetops deploy a haze of
cherry bloom for roots,
where birds coast belly-up
in the glass bowl of a hill;
from its bottom a bunch
of peanut-munching children
are suspended by their
sneakers, waveringly.

A swan, with twin necks
forming the figure three,
steers between two dimpled
towers doubled. Fondly
hissing, she kisses herself,
and all the scene is troubled:
water-windows splinter,
tree-limbs tangle, the bridge
folds like a fan.

MAY SWENSON

The Marsh

Swampstrife and spatterdock
    lull in the heavy waters;
some thirty little frogs
    spring with each step you walk;
a fish's belly glitters
    tangled near rotting logs.

Over by the gray rocks
    muskrats dip and circle.
Out of his rim of ooze
    a silt-black pond snail walks
inverted on the surface
    toward what food he may choose.

You look up; while you walk
    the sun bobs and is snarled
in the enclosing weir
    of trees, in their dead stalks.
Stick in the mud, old heart,
    what are you doing here?

W. D. SNODGRASS

A Blaze of Noons

Summer's Sweetness

Long Summer

Gold as an infant's humming dream,
Stamped with its timeless, tropic blush,
The steady sun stands in the air
And burns like Moses' holy bush.

And burns while nothing it consumes;
The smoking branch but greener grows,
The crackling briar, from budded lips,
A floating stream of blossom blows.

A daze of hours, a blaze of noons,
Licks my cold shadow from the ground;
A flaming trident rears each dawn
To stir the blood of earth around.

Unsinged beneath the furnace sky
The frenzied beetle runs reborn,
The ant his antic mountain moves,
The rampant ram rewinds his horn.

I see the crazy bees drop fat
From tulips ten times gorged and dry;
I see the sated swallow plunge
To drink the dazzled waterfly.

A halo flares around my head,
A sunflower flares across the sun,
While down the summer's seamless haze
Such feasts of milk and honey run

That lying with my orchid love,
Whose kiss no frost of age can sever,
I cannot doubt the cold is dead,
The gold earth turned to good—forever.

LAURIE LEE

Let Us Go, Then, Exploring

Let us go, then, exploring
This summer morning,
When all are adoring
The plum blossom and the bee.
And humming and hawing
Let us ask of the starling
What he may think
On the brink
Of the dustbin whence he picks
Among the sticks
Combings of scullion's hair.
What's life, we ask;
Life, Life, Life! cries the bird
As if he had heard. . . .

VIRGINIA WOOLF

Summer

Winter is cold-hearted,
Spring is yea and nay,
Autumn is a weathercock
    Blown every way.
Summer days for me
When every leaf is on its tree;

When Robin's not a beggar,
And Jenny Wren's a bride,
And larks hang singing, singing, singing
    Over the wheat fields wide,
    And anchored lilies ride,
    And the pendulum spider
    Swings from side to side;

And blue-black beetles transact business,
    And gnats fly in a host,
And furry caterpillars hasten
    That no time be lost,
    And moths grow fat and thrive,
    And ladybirds arrive.

Before green apples blush,
Before green nuts embrown,
Why one day in the country
Is worth a month in town;
Is worth a day and a year
Of the dusty, musty, lag-last fashion
    That days drone elsewhere.

CHRISTINA ROSSETTI

Discovering God Is Waking One Morning

Discovering God is waking one morning
sun beaming, an east wind blowing,

bees humming on Queen Anne's lace,
lace tilting, bowing in the wind,

and knowing there is more than this.
Now everything is different, better.

The morning sun laughing at shadows
east wind blowing smiles from the sea

Queen Anne bowing greeting in the meadow;
my whole world sings a hymn, awaking.

JOHN L'HEUREUX

A Midsummer Song

O, father's gone to market town, he was up before the day,
And Jamie's after robins, and the man is making hay,
And whistling down the hollow goes the boy that minds
    the mill,
While mother from the kitchen door is calling with a will:
    "Polly!—Polly!—The cows are in the corn!
    O, where's Polly?"

From all the misty morning air there comes a summer
    sound—
A murmur as of waters from skies and trees and ground.
The birds they sing upon the wing, the pigeons bill and coo,

And over hill and hollow rings again the loud halloo:
  "Polly!—Polly!—The cows are in the corn!
  O, where's Polly?"

Above the trees the honeybees swarm by with buzz and
    boom,
And in the field and garden a thousand blossoms bloom.
Within the farmer's meadow a brown-eyed daisy blows,
And down at the edge of the hollow a red and thorny
    rose.
  But Polly!—Polly!—The cows are in the corn!
  O, where's Polly?

How strange at such a time of day the mill should stop
    its clatter!
The farmer's wife is listening now and wonders what's
    the matter.
O, wild the birds are singing in the wood and on the hill,
While whistling up the hollow goes the boy that minds
    the mill.
  But Polly!—Polly!—The cows are in the corn!
  O, where's Polly?

RICHARD WATSON GILDER

Zummer Stream

    Ah! then the grassy-meäded Maÿ
    Did warm the passèn year, an' gleam
    Upon the yollow-grounded stream,
    That still by beech-tree sheädes do straÿ.
    The light o' weäves, a-runnèn there,
        Did plaÿ on leaves up over head,
    An' vishes sceäly zides did gleäre,
        A-dartèn on the shallow bed,
    An' like the stream a-slidèn on,
    My zun out-measur'd time's agone.

There by the path, in grass knee-high,
Wer buttervlees in giddy flight,
All white above the deäisies white,
Or blue below the deep blue sky.
Then glowèn warm wer ev'ry brow,
O' maïd, or man, in zummer het,
An' warm did glow the cheäks I met
That time, noo mwore to meet em now.
As brooks, a-slidèn on their bed,
My season-measur'd time's a-vled.

Vrom yonder window, in the thatch,
Did sound the maïdens' merry words,
As I did stand, by zingèn birds,
Bezide the elem-sheäded hatch.
'Tis good to come back to the pleäce,
    Back to the time, to goo noo mwore;
'Tis good to meet the younger feäce
    A-mentèn others here avore.
As streams do glide by green mead-grass,
My zummer-brighten'd years do pass.

WILLIAM BARNES

Weekend Stroll

Step to the garden from the cool-roomed house;
What sun-hot grass; what Canterbury Bells:
How rich along the lane the rustic smells
Of flowering elder and of hidden cows;
What buzzing happy silence where they browse;
What wealth of caverned shade among the
    boughs,
What breadth of light on the receiving corn!
July is born.

FRANCES CORNFORD

Summer

How sweet, when weary, dropping on a bank,
    Turning a look around on things that be!
E'en feather-headed grasses, spindling rank,
    A-trembling to the breeze one loves to see;
    And yellow buttercup, where many a bee
Comes buzzing to its head and bows it down;
    And the great dragonfly with gauzy wings,
In gilded coat of purple, green, or brown,
    That on broad leaves of hazel basking clings,
    Fond of the sunny day—and other things
Past counting, please me while thus here I lie.
    But still reflective pains are not forgot:
Summer sometime shall bless this spot, when I,
    Hapt in the cold dark grave, can heed it not.

                                        JOHN CLARE

The Schoolboy

I love to rise in a summer morn
When the birds sing on every tree;
The distant huntsman winds his horn,
And the skylark sings with me.
O! what sweet company.

But to go to school in a summer morn,
O! it drives all joy away;
Under a cruel eye outworn,
The little ones spend the day
In sighing and dismay.

Ah! then at times I drooping sit,
And spend many an anxious hour,
Nor in my book can I take delight,
Nor sit in learning's bower,
Worn thro' with the dreary shower.

How can the bird that is born for joy
Sit in a cage and sing?
How can a child, when fears annoy,
But droop his tender wing,
And forget his youthful spring?

O! father and mother, if buds are nip'd
And blossoms blown away,
And if the tender plants are strip'd
Of their joy in the springing day,
By sorrow and care's dismay,

How shall the summer arise in joy,
Or the summer fruits appear?
Or how shall we gather what griefs destroy,
Or bless the mellowing year,
When the blasts of winter appear?

WILLIAM BLAKE

Midsummer Jingle

I've an ingle, shady ingle, near a dusky bosky dingle
Where the sighing zephyrs mingle with the purling of
the stream.
There I linger in the jungle, and it makes me thrill and
tingle,
Far from city's strident jangle as I angle, smoke and
dream.

Through the trees I'll hear a single ringing sound, a
cowbell's jingle,
And its ting-a-ling'll mingle with the whispers of the
breeze;
So, although I've not a single sou, no potentate or king'll
Make me jealous while I angle in my ingle 'neath the
trees.

NEWMAN LEVY

In Fields of Summer

The sun rises,
The goldenrod blooms,
I drift in fields of summer,
My life is adrift in my body,
It shines in my heart and hands, in my teeth,
It shines up at the old crane
Who holds out his drainpipe of a neck
And creaks along in the blue,

And the goldenrod shines with its life, too,
And the grass, look,
The great field wavers and flakes,
The rumble of bumblebees keeps deepening,
A phoebe flutters up,
A lark bursts up all dew.

GALWAY KINNELL

The Throstle

"Summer is coming, summer is coming,
    I know it, I know it, I know it.
Light again, leaf again, life again, love again,"
    Yes, my wild little Poet.

Sing the new year in under the blue,
    Last year you sang it as gladly.
"New, new, new, new"! Is it then *so* new
    That you should carol so madly?

"Love again, song again, nest again, young again,"
    Never a prophet so crazy!
And hardly a daisy as yet, little friend,
    See, there is hardly a daisy.

"Here again, here, here, here, happy year"!
O warble unchidden, unbidden!
Summer is coming, is coming, my dear,
And all the winters are hidden.

ALFRED, LORD TENNYSON

Summer Afternoon

To zig-zag with the ant
through grass-topped jungles, sway
in many-masted trees with birds, hang fluttering
over the tiger lilies with the lone
white butterfly,
                           anything, anything
but sitting here sheltered from the sun,

while all around me the summer
burns, beats, and blazes
from sun to sky to green—

hot, naked, unashamed beauty!

RAYMOND SOUSTER

Sunday at the End of Summer

Last night the cold wind and the rain blew
Hard from the west, all night, until the creek
Flooded, tearing the end of a wooden bridge
Down to hang, trembling, in the violent water.

This morning, with the weather still in rage,
I watched workmen already at repairs.
Some hundred of us came around to watch,
With collars turned against the rain and wind.

Down the wild water, where men stood to the knees,
We saw come flooding hollyhock and vine,
Sunflowers tall and broken, thorny bramble
And pale lilies cracked along the stalk.

Ours was the Sunday's perfect idleness
To watch those others working; who fought, swore,
Being threshed at hip and thigh, against that trash
Of pale wild flowers and their drifting legs.

HOWARD NEMEROV

The Deceptive Present, The Phoenix Year

As I looked, the poplar rose in the shining air
Like a slender throat,
And there was an exaltation of flowers,
The surf of apple tree delicately foaming.

All winter, the trees had been
Silent soldiers, a vigil of woods,
Their hidden feelings
Scrawled and became
Scores of black vines,
Barbed wire sharp against the ice-white sky.
Who could believe then
In the green, glittering vividness of full-leafed summer?
Who will be able to believe, when winter again begins
After the autumn burns down again, and the day is
    ashen,
And all returns to winter and winter's ashes,
Wet, white, ice, wooden, dulled and dead, brittle or
    frozen,
Who will believe or feel in mind and heart
The reality of the spring and of birth,
In the green warm opulence of summer, and the
    inexhaustible vitality and immortality of the earth?

DELMORE SCHWARTZ

Summer

Glow-worm-like the daisies peer;
    Roses in the thickets fade,
Grudging every petal dear;
    Swinging incense in the shade
The honeysuckle's chandelier
    Twinkles down a shadowy glade.

Now is Nature's restful mood:
    Death-still stands the somber fir;
Hardly where the rushes brood
    Something crawling makes a stir;
Hardly in the underwood
    Russet pinions softly whir.

JOHN DAVIDSON

Blackberry–picking

For Philip Hobsbaum

Late August, given heavy rain and sun
For a full week, the blackberries would ripen.
At first, just one, a glossy purple clot
Among others, red, green, hard as a knot.
You ate that first one and its flesh was sweet
Like thickened wine: summer's blood was in it
Leaving stains upon the tongue and lust for
Picking. Then red ones inked up and that hunger
Sent us out with milk cans, pea tins, jam pots
Where briars scratched and wet grass bleached our boots.
Round hayfields, cornfields and potato drills
We trekked and picked until the cans were full,
Until the tinkling bottom had been covered
With green ones, and on top big dark blobs burned
Like a plate of eyes. Our hands were peppered

With thorn pricks, our palms sticky as Bluebeard's.

We hoarded the fresh berries in the byre.
But when the bath was filled we found a fur,
A rat-gray fungus, glutting on our cache.
The juice was stinking too. Once off the bush
The fruit fermented, the sweet flesh would turn sour.
I always felt like crying. It wasn't fair
That all the lovely canfuls smelt of rot.
Each year I hoped they'd keep, knew they would not.

SEAMUS HEANEY

Summer and Winter

It was a bright and cheerful afternoon,
Toward the end of the sunny month of June,
When the north wind congregates in crowds
The floating mountains of the silver clouds
From the horizon—and the stainless sky
Opens beyond them like eternity.
All things rejoiced beneath the sun; the weeds,
The river, and the cornfields, and the reeds;
The willow leaves that glanced in the light breeze,
And the firm foliage of the larger trees.

It was a winter such as when birds die
In the deep forests; and the fishes lie
Stiffened in the translucent ice, which makes
Even the mud and slime of the warm lakes
A wrinkled clod as hard as brick; and when,
Among their children, comfortable men
Gather about great fires, and yet feel cold:
Alas, then, for the homeless beggar old!

PERCY BYSSHE SHELLEY

Summer Shower

A drop fell on the apple tree,
Another on the roof;
A half a dozen kissed the eaves,
And made the gables laugh.

A few went out to help the brook,
That went to help the sea.
Myself conjectured, Were they pearls,
What necklaces could be!

The dust replaced in hoisted roads,
The birds jocoser sung;
The sunshine threw his hat away,
The orchards spangles hung.

The breezes brought dejected lutes,
And bathed them in the glee;
The East put out a single flag,
And signed the fête away.

EMILY DICKINSON

The End of Summer

When poppies in the garden bleed,
And coreopsis goes to seed,
And pansies, blossoming past their prime,
Grow small and smaller all the time,
When on the mown field, shrunk and dry,
Brown dock and purple thistle lie,
And smoke from forest fires at noon
Can make the sun appear the moon,
When apple seeds, all white before,

Begin to darken in the core,
I know that summer, scarcely here,
Is gone until another year.

EDNA ST. VINCENT MILLAY

Exeunt

Piecemeal the summer dies;
At the field's edge a daisy lives alone;
A last shawl of burning lies
On a gray field-stone.

All cries are thin and terse;
The field has droned the summer's final mass;
A cricket like a dwindled hearse
Crawls from the dry grass.

RICHARD WILBUR

Wait for the Moon to Rise

Night, Stars, and the Moon

If the Owl Calls Again

at dusk
from the island in the river
and it's not too cold,

I'll wait for the moon
to rise,

then take wing and glide
to meet him.

We will not speak,
but hooded against the frost
soar above
the alder flats, searching
with tawny eyes.

And then we'll sit
in the shadowy spruce and
pick the bones
of careless mice,

while the long moon drifts
toward Asia
and the river mutters
in its icy bed.

And when morning climbs
the limbs
we'll part without a sound,

fulfilled, floating
homeward as
the cold world awakens.

JOHN HAINES

Village Before Sunset

There is a moment country children know
When half across the field the shadows go
And even the birds sing leisurely and slow.

There's timelessness in every passing tread;
Even the far-off train as it puffs ahead,
Even the voices calling them to bed.

FRANCES CORNFORD

The Midges Dance Aboon the Burn

The midges dance aboon the burn;
   The dews begin to fa';
The paitricks doun the rushy holm
   Set up their e'ening ca'.
Now loud and clear the blackbird's sang
   Rings through the briery shaw,
While, flitting gay, the swallows play
   Around the castle wa'.

Beneath the golden gloamin' sky
    The mavis mends her lay;
The redbreast pours his sweetest strains
    To charm the lingering day;
While weary yeldrins seem to wail
    Their little nestlings torn;
The merry wren, frae den to den,
    Gaes jinking through the thorn.

The roses fauld their silken leaves,
    The foxglove shuts its bell;
The honeysuckle and the birk
    Spread fragrance through the dell.—
Let others crowd the giddy court
    Of mirth and revelry,
The simple joys that Nature yields
    Are dearer far to me.

ROBERT TANNAHILL

Twilight Calm

Oh pleasant eventide!
Clouds on the western side
Grow gray and grayer, hiding the warm sun:
The bees and birds, their happy labors done,
    Seek their close nests and bide.

Screened in the leafy wood
The stock doves sit and brood:
The very squirrel leaps from bough to bough
But lazily; pauses; and settles now
    Where once he stored his food.

One by one the flowers close,
　　Lily and dewy rose
Shutting their tender petals from the moon:
The grasshoppers are still; but not so soon
　　Are still the noisy crows.

　　The dormouse squats and eats
　　Choice little dainty bits
Beneath the spreading roots of a broad lime;
Nibbling his fill he stops from time to time
　　And listens where he sits.

　　From far the lowings come
　　Of cattle driven home:
From farther still the wind brings fitfully
The vast continual murmur of the sea,
　　Now loud, now almost dumb.

　　The gnats whirl in the air,
　　The evening gnats; and there
The owl opes broad his eyes and wings to sail
For prey; the bat wakes; and the shell-less snail
　　Comes forth, clammy and bare.

　　Hark! that's the nightingale,
　　Telling the selfsame tale
Her song told when this ancient earth was young:
So echoes answered when her song was sung
　　In the first wooded vale.

　　In separate herds the deer
　　Lie; here the bucks, and here
The does, and by its mother sleeps the fawn:
Through all the hours of night until the dawn
　　They sleep, forgetting fear.

The hare sleeps where it lies,
    With wary half-closed eyes;
The cock has ceased to crow, the hen to cluck:
Only the fox is out, some heedless duck
    Or chicken to surprise.

Remote, each single star
    Comes out, till there they are
All shining brightly. How the dews fall damp!
While close at hand the glowworm lights her lamp,
    Or twinkles from afar.

But evening now is done
    As much as if the sun
Day-giving had arisen in the East—
For night has come; and the great calm has ceased,
    The quiet sands have run.

CHRISTINA ROSSETTI

Night

The sun descending in the west,
The evening star does shine;
The birds are silent in their nest,
And I must seek for mine.
The moon like a flower
In heaven's high bower,
With silent delight
Sits and smiles on the night.

Farewell, green fields and happy groves,
Where flocks have took delight.
Where lambs have nibbled, silent moves
The feet of angels bright;
Unseen they pour blessing
And joy without ceasing
On each bud and blossom,
And each sleeping bosom.

They look in every thoughtless nest,
Where birds are cover'd warm;
They visit caves of every beast,
To keep them all from harm.
If they see any weeping
That should have been sleeping,
They pour sleep on their head,
And sit down by their bed.

When wolves and tigers howl for prey,
They pitying stand and weep;
Seeking to drive their thirst away,
And keep them from the sheep;
But if they rush dreadful,
The angels, most heedful,
Receive each mild spirit,
New worlds to inherit.

And there the lion's ruddy eyes
Shall flow with tears of gold,
And pitying the tender cries,
And walking round the fold,
Saying "Wrath, by his meekness,
And by his health, sickness
Is driven away
From our immortal day.

And now beside thee, bleating lamb,
I can lie down and sleep;
Or think on him who bore thy name,
Graze after thee and weep.
For wash'd in life's river,
My bright mane forever
Shall shine like the gold
As I guard o'er the fold."

WILLIAM BLAKE

Stone Trees

Last night a sword-light in the sky
Flashed a swift terror on the dark.
In that sharp light the fields did lie
Naked and stonelike; each tree stood
Like a tranced woman, bound and stark.
      Far off the wood
With darkness ridged the riven dark.

And cows astonished stared with fear,
And sheep crept to the knees of cows,
And conies to their burrows slid,
And rooks were still in rigid boughs,
And all things else were still or hid.
      From all the wood
Came but the owl's hoot, ghostly, clear.

In that cold trance the earth was held
It seemed an age, or time was nought.
Sure never from that stonelike field
Sprang golden corn, nor from those chill
Gray granite trees was music wrought.
      In all the wood
Even the tall poplar hung stone still.

It seemed an age, or time was none . . .
Slowly the earth heaved out of sleep
And shivered, and the trees of stone
Bent and sighed in the gusty wind,
And rain swept as birds flocking sweep.
      Far off the wood
Rolled the slow thunders on the wind.

From all the wood came no brave bird,
No song broke through the close-fall'n night,
Nor any sound from cowering herd:
Only a dog's long lonely howl
When from the window poured pale light.
      And from the wood
The hoot came ghostly of the owl.

JOHN FREEMAN

To the Evening Star

Thou fair-hair'd angel of the evening,
Now, whilst the sun rests on the mountains, light
Thy bright torch of love; thy radiant crown
Put on, and smile upon our evening bed!
Smile on our loves, and, while thou drawest the
Blue curtains of the sky, scatter thy silver dew
On every flower that shuts its sweet eyes
In timely sleep. Let thy west wind sleep on
The lake; speak silence with thy glimmering eyes,
And wash the dusk with silver. Soon, full soon,
Dost thou withdraw; then the wolf rages wide,
And the lion glares thro' the dun forest:
The fleeces of our flocks are cover'd with
Thy sacred dew: protect them with thine influence.

WILLIAM BLAKE

Star-talk

"Are you awake, Gemelli,
    This frosty night?"
"We'll be awake till reveillé,
Which is Sunrise," say the Gemelli,
"It's no good trying to go to sleep:
If there's wine to be got we'll drink it deep,
    But rest is hopeless tonight,
    But rest is hopeless tonight."

"Are you cold too, poor Pleiads,
    This frosty night?"
"Yes, and so are the Hyads:
See us cuddle and hug," say the Pleiads,
"All six in a ring: it keeps us warm:
We huddle together like birds in a storm:
    It's bitter weather tonight,
    It's bitter weather tonight."

"What do you hunt, Orion,
    This starry night?"
"The Ram, the Bull, and the Lion,
And the Great Bear," says Orion,
"With my starry quiver and beautiful belt
I am trying to find a good thick pelt
    To warm my shoulders tonight,
    To warm my shoulders tonight."

"Did you hear that, Great She-bear,
    This frosty night?"
"Yes, he's talking of stripping *me* bare
Of my own big fur," says the She-bear.
"I'm afraid of the man and his terrible arrow:
The thought of it chills my bones to the marrow,
    And the frost so cruel tonight!
    And the frost so cruel tonight!"

"How is your trade, Aquarius,
    This frosty night?"
"Complaints are many and various
And my feet are cold," says Aquarius,
"There's Venus objects to Dolphin-scales,
And Mars to Crab-spawn found in my pails,
    And the pump has frozen tonight,
    And the pump has frozen tonight."

ROBERT GRAVES

The Full Heart

Alone on the shore in the pause of the nighttime
I stand and I hear the long wind blow light;
I view the constellations quietly, quietly burning;
I hear the wave fall in the hush of the night.

Long after I am dead, ended this bitter journey,
Many another whose heart holds no light
Shall your solemn sweetness hush, awe and comfort,
O my companions, Wind, Water, Stars, and Night.

ROBERT NICHOLS

The Sound of Night

And now the dark comes on, all full of chitter noise.
Birds huggermugger crowd the trees,
the air thick with their vesper cries,
and bats, snub seven-pointed kites,
skitter across the lake, swing out,
squeak, chirp, dip, and skim on skates
of air, and the fat frogs wake and prink
wide-lipped, noisy as ducks, drunk
on the boozy black, gloating chink-chunk.

And now on the narrow beach we defend ourselves from dark.
The cooking done, we build our firework
bright and hot and less for outlook
than for magic, and lie in our blankets
while night nickers around us. Crickets
chorus hallelujahs; paws, quiet
and quick as raindrops, play on the stones
expertly soft, run past and are gone;
fish pulse in the lake; the frogs hoarsen.

Now every voice of the hour—the known, the supposed,
    the strange,
the mindless, the witted, the never seen—
sing, thrum, impinge, and rearrange
endlessly; and debarred from sleep we wait
for the birds, importantly silent,
for the crease of first eye-licking light,
for the sun, lost long ago and sweet.
By the lake, locked black away and tight,
we lie, day creatures, overhearing night.

MAXINE W. KUMIN

Back Yard, July Night

Firefly, airplane, satellite, star—
How I wonder which you are.

WILLIAM COLE

Welcome to the Moon

Welcome, precious stone of the night,
Delight of the skies, precious stone of the night,
Mother of stars, precious stone of the night,
Excellency of stars, precious stone of the night.

(from the Gaelic)

Night Airs

Night airs that make tree shadows walk, and sheep
Washed white in the cold moonshine on gray cliffs.

WALTER SAVAGE LANDOR

Full Moon

One night as Dick lay fast asleep,
    Into his drowsy eyes
A great still light began to creep
    From out the silent skies.
It was the lovely moon's, for when
    He raised his dreamy head,
Her surge of silver filled the pane
    And streamed across his bed.
So, for a while, each gazed at each—
    Dick and the solemn moon—
Till, climbing slowly on her way,
    She vanished, and was gone.

WALTER DE LA MARE

Aware

Slowly the moon is rising out of the ruddy haze,
Divesting herself of her golden shift, and so
Emerging white and exquisite; and I in amaze
See in the sky before me, a woman I did not know
I loved, but there she goes, and her beauty hurts my
    heart;
I follow her down the night, begging her not to depart.

D. H. LAWRENCE

It Was the Lovely Moon

It was the lovely moon—she lifted
Slowly her white brow among
Bronze cloud-waves that ebbed and drifted
Faintly, faintlier afar.
Calm she looked, yet pale with wonder,
Sweet in unwonted thoughtfulness,
Watching the earth that dwindled under
Faintly, faintlier afar.
It was the lovely moon that lovelike
Hovered over the wandering, tired
Earth, her bosom gray and dovelike,
Hovering beautiful as a dove. . . .
The lovely moon: —her soft light falling
Lightly on roof and poplar and pine—
Tree to tree whispering and calling,
Wonderful in the silvery shine
Of the round, lovely, thoughtful moon.

JOHN FREEMAN

To the Moon

"What have you looked at, Moon,
      In your time,
   Now long past your prime?"
"O, I have looked at, often looked at
      Sweet, sublime,
Sore things, shudderful, night and noon
      In my time."

"What have you mused on, Moon,
    In your day,
    So aloof, so far away?"
"O, I have mused on, often mused on
        Growth, decay,
Nations alive, dead, mad, aswoon,
        In my day!"

"Have you much wondered, Moon,
    On your rounds,
    Self-wrapt, beyond Earth's bounds?"
Yea, I have wondered, often wondered
        At the sounds
Reaching me of the human tune
        On my rounds."

"What do you think of it, Moon,
        As you go?
    Is Life much, or no?"
"O, I think of it, often think of it
        As a show
God ought surely to shut up soon,
        As I go."

THOMAS HARDY

To the Moon

Art thou pale for weariness
    Of climbing heaven and gazing on the earth,
Wandering companionless
Among the stars that have a different birth—
And ever changing, like a joyless eye
That finds no object worth its constancy?

PERCY BYSSHE SHELLEY

Silver

Slowly, silently, now the moon
Walks the night in her silver shoon;
This way, and that, she peers, and sees
Silver fruit upon silver trees;
One by one the casements catch
Her beams beneath the silvery thatch;
Couched in his kennel, like a log,
With paws of silver sleeps the dog;
From their shadowy cote the white breasts peep
Of doves in a silver-feathered sleep;
A harvest mouse goes scampering by,
With silver claws, and silver eye;
And moveless fish in the water gleam,
By silver reeds in a silver stream.

WALTER DE LA MARE

The Languishing Moon

With how sad steps, O Moon, thou climb'st the skies!
How silently, and with how wan a face!
What, may it be that even in heavenly place
That busy archer his sharp arrows tries—
Sure, if that long with love-acquainted eyes
Can judge of love, thou feel'st a lover's case?
I read it in thy looks; thy languished grace,
To me that feel the like, thy state descries.
Then, even of fellowship, O Moon, tell me,
Is constant love deemed there but want of wit?
Are beauties there as proud as here they be?
Do they above love to be loved, and yet
    Those lovers scorn whom that love doth possess
    Do they call virtue there, ungratefulness?

SIR PHILIP SIDNEY

New Moon

The new moon, of no importance
lingers behind as the yellow sun glares and is gone
    beyond the sea's edge;
earth smokes blue;
the new moon, in cool height above the blushes,
brings a fresh fragrance of heaven to our senses.

D. H. LAWRENCE

In Dispraise of the Moon

I would not be the Moon, the sickly thing,
To summon owls and bats upon the wing;
For when the noble Sun is gone away,
She turns his night into a pallid day.

She hath no air, no radiance of her own,
That world unmusical of earth and stone.
She wakes her dim, uncolored, voiceless hosts,
Ghost of the Sun, herself the sun of ghosts.

The mortal eyes that gaze too long on her
Of Reason's piercing ray defrauded are.
Light in itself doth feed the living brain;
That light, reflected, but makes darkness plain.

MARY COLERIDGE

The Early Morning

The moon on the one hand, the dawn on the other:
The moon is my sister, the dawn is my brother.
The moon on my left and the dawn on my right.
My brother, good morning: my sister, good night.

HILAIRE BELLOC

Season of Mists and Mellow Fruitfulness

Autumn and Harvest

To Autumn

Season of mists and mellow fruitfulness,
    Close bosom friend of the maturing sun;
Conspiring with him how to load and bless
    With fruit the vines that round the thatch eaves run;
To bend with apples the moss'd cottage trees,
    And fill all fruit with ripeness to the core;
    To swell the gourd, and plump the hazel shells
    With a sweet kernel; to set budding more,
And still more, later flowers for the bees,
Until they think warm days will never cease,
    For Summer has o'er-brimmed their clammy cells.

Who hath not seen thee oft amid thy store?
    Sometimes whoever seeks abroad may find
Thee sitting careless on a granary floor,
    Thy hair soft-lifted by the winnowing wind;
Or on a half-reap'd furrow sound asleep,
    Drows'd with the fume of poppies, while thy hook
        Spares the next swath and all its twined flowers:
And sometimes like a gleaner thou dost keep
    Steady thy laden head across a brook;
    Or by a cider press, with patient look,
        Thou watchest the last oozings hours by hours.

Where are the songs of Spring? Aye, where are they?
　　Think not of them, thou hast thy music too,—
While barred clouds bloom the soft-dying day,
　　And touch the stubble plains with rosy hue;
Then in a wailful choir the small gnats mourn
　　Among the river sallows, borne aloft
　　　　Or sinking as the light wind lives or dies;
And full-grown lambs loud bleat from hilly bourn;
　　Hedge crickets sing; and now with treble soft
The redbreast whistles from a garden croft;
　　And gathering swallows twitter in the skies.

JOHN KEATS

The Ripe and Bearded Barley

Come out, 'tis now September,
　　The hunter's moon's begun;
And through the wheaten stubble
　　We hear the frequent gun;
The leaves are turning yellow,
　　And fading into red,
While the ripe and bearded barley
　　Is hanging down its head.

　　　All among the barley,
　　　　Who would not be blithe,
　　　While the ripe and bearded barley
　　　　Is smiling on the scythe!

The wheat is like a rich man,
　　It's sleek and well-to-do;
The oats are like a pack of girls,
　　They're thin and dancing too,
The rye is like a miser,
　　Both sulky, lean, and small,
Whilst the ripe and bearded barley
　　Is the monarch of them all.

All among the barley,
Who would not be blithe,
While the ripe and bearded barley
Is smiling on the scythe!

The spring is like a young maid
    That does not know her mind,
The summer is a tyrant
    Of most ungracious kind;
The autumn is an old friend
    That pleases all he can,
And brings the bearded barley
    To glad the heart of man.

All among the barley,
Who would not be blithe,
When the ripe and bearded barley
Is smiling on the scythe!

ANONYMOUS

Ode to the West Wind

O wild West Wind, thou breath of Autumn's being,
    Thou from whose unseen presence the leaves dead
Are driven like ghosts from an enchanter fleeing,
    Yellow, and black, and pale, and hectic red,
Pestilence-stricken multitudes! O thou
    Who chariotest to their dark wintry bed
The wingèd seeds, where they lie cold and low,
    Each like a corpse within its grave, until
Thine azure sister of the Spring shall blow
    Her clarion o'er the dreaming earth, and fill
(Driving sweet buds like flocks to feed in air)
    With living hues and odors plain and hill:
Wild Spirit which art moving everywhere;
Destroyer and preserver; hear, oh hear!

Thou on whose stream, 'mid the steep sky's commotion,
　　Loose clouds like earth's decaying leaves are shed,
Shook from the tangled boughs of heaven and ocean,
　　Angels of rain and lightning: there are spread
On the blue surface of thine airy surge,
　　Like the bright hair uplifted from the head
Of some fierce Mænad, even from the dim verge
　　Of the horizon to the zenith's height,
The locks of the approaching storm. Thou dirge
　　Of the dying year, to which this closing night
Will be the dome of a vast sepulcher,
　　Vaulted with all thy congregated might
Of vapors, from whose solid atmosphere
Black rain, and fire, and hail, will burst: Oh hear!

Thou who didst waken from his summer dreams
　　The blue Mediterranean, where he lay,
Lulled by the coil of his crystalline streams,
　　Beside a pumice isle in Baiæ's bay,
And saw in sleep old palaces and towers
　　Quivering within the wave's intenser day,
All overgrown with azure moss, and flowers
　　So sweet the sense faints picturing them! Thou
For whose path the Atlantic's level powers
　　Cleave themselves into chasms, while far below
The sea-blooms and the oozy woods which wear
　　The sapless foliage of the ocean know
Thy voice, and suddenly grow gray with fear,
And tremble and despoil themselves: Oh, hear!

If I were a dead leaf thou mightest bear;
　　If I were a swift cloud to fly with thee;
A wave to pant beneath thy power, and share
　　The impulse of thy strength, only less free
Than thou, O uncontrollable! if even
　　I were as in my boyhood, and could be
The comrade of thy wanderings over heaven,

As then, when to outstrip thy skyey speed
Scarce seemed a vision,—I would ne'er have striven
    As thus with thee in prayer in my sore need.
Oh, lift me as a wave, a leaf, a cloud!
    I fall upon the thorns of life! I bleed!
A heavy weight of hours has chained and bowed
One too like thee—tameless, and swift, and proud.

Make me thy lyre, even as the forest is:
    What if my leaves are falling like its own?
The tumult of thy mighty harmonies
    Will take from both a deep autumnal tone,
Sweet though in sadness. Be thou, Spirit fierce,
    My spirit! Be thou me, impetuous one!
Drive my dead thoughts over the universe,
    Like withered leaves, to quicken a new birth;
And, by the incantation of this verse,
    Scatter, as from an unextinguished hearth
Ashes and sparks, my words among mankind!
    Be through my lips to unawakened earth
The trumpet of a prophecy! O Wind,
If Winter comes, can Spring be far behind?

PERCY BYSSHE SHELLEY

Autumn

The morns are meeker than they were,
The nuts are getting brown;
The berry's cheek is plumper,
The rose is out of town.

The maple wears a gayer scarf,
The field a scarlet gown.
Lest I should be old-fashioned,
I'll put a trinket on.

EMILY DICKINSON

Hurrahing in Harvest

Summer ends now; now, barbarous in beauty, the stooks
    arise
    Around; up above, what wind-walks! what lovely
      behavior
    Of silk-sack clouds! has wilder, wilful-wavier
Meal-drift molded ever and melted across skies?

I walk, I lift up, I lift up heart, eyes,
    Down all that glory in the heavens to glean our
      Saviour;
    And, eyes, heart, what looks, what lips yet gave you a
Rapturous love's greeting of realer, of rounder replies?

And the azurous hung hills are his world-wielding
      shoulder
    Majestic—as a stallion stalwart, very-violet-sweet!—
These things, these things were here and but the
      beholder
    Wanting; which two when they once meet,
The heart rears wings bold and bolder
    And hurls for him, O half hurls earth for him off
      under his feet.

GERARD MANLEY HOPKINS

The Autumn Wind

The autumn's wind on suthering wings
    Plays round the oak tree strong
And through the hawthorn hedges sings
    The year's departing song.
There's every leaf upon the whirl
    Ten thousand times an hour,
The grassy meadows crisp and curl
    With here and there a flower.

There's nothing in this world I find
But wakens to the autumn wind.

The chaffinch flies from out the bushes,
    The bluecap "teehees" on the tree,
The wind sues on in merry gushes
    His murmuring autumn minstrelsy.
The robin sings his autumn song
    Upon the crab tree overhead,
The clouds of smoke they sail along,
    Leaves rustle from their mossy bed.
There's nothing suits my musing mind
Like to the pleasant autumn wind.

How many a mile it suthers on
    And stays to dally with the leaves,
And when the first broad blast is gone
    A stranger gust the foliage heaves.
The poplar tree is turned to gray
    And crowds of leaves do by it ride,
The birch tree dances all the day
    In concert with the rippling tide.
There's nothing calms the unquiet mind
Like to the soothing autumn's wind.

Sweet twittering o'er the meadow grass,
    Soft sueing o'er the fallow ground,
The lark starts up as on they pass
    With many a gush and moaning sound.
It fans the feathers of the bird
    And ruffles robin's ruddy breast
As round the hovel's end it swerved,
    Then sobs and sighs and goes to rest.
In solitude the musing mind
Must ever love the autumn wind.

JOHN CLARE

Moonlit Apples

At the top of the house the apples are laid in rows,
And the skylight lets the moonlight in, and those
Apples are deep-sea apples of green. There goes
    A cloud on the moon in the autumn night.

A mouse in the wainscot scratches, and scratches, and
      then
There is no sound at the top of the house of men
Or mice; and the cloud is blown, and the moon again
    Dapples the apples with deep-sea light.

They are lying in rows there, under the gloomy beams;
On the sagging floor; they gather the silver streams
Out of the moon, those moonlit apples of dreams,
    And quiet is the steep stair under.

In the corridors under there is nothing but sleep,
And stiller than ever on orchard boughs they keep
Tryst with the moon, and deep is the silence, deep
    On moon-washed apples of wonder.

JOHN DRINKWATER

Autumn Scene

Here on the mellow hill
    I sit content with Autumn and as still
To watch a man in the valley felling an oak tree.
    Diminished by the distance to a boy,
He swings the ax, his toy:
    And while I wonder how
Such seeming gentle blows could end an oak,
    After each silent stroke,
As if from a doomed twig or bough
    That ax had set it free,
The sound floats upward like a bird to me.

BASIL DOWLING

Song

The feathers of the willow
Are half of them grown yellow
    Above the swelling stream;
And ragged are the bushes,
And rusty now the rushes,
    And wild the clouded gleam.

The thistle now is older,
His stalk begins to moulder,
    His head is white as snow;
The branches all are barer,
The linnet's song is rarer,
    The robin pipeth now.

RICHARD WATSON DIXON

When the Frost Is on the Punkin

When the frost is on the punkin and the fodder's in the
    shock,
And you hear the kyouck and gobble of the struttin'
    turkey cock,
And the clakin' of the guineys, and the cluckin' of the hens,
And the rooster's hallylooer as he tiptoes on the fence;
O it's then's the times a feller is a-feelin' at his best,
With the risin' sun to greet him from a night of
    peaceful rest,
As he leaves the house, bare headed, and goes out to feed
    the stock,
When the frost is on the punkin and the fodder's in the
    shock.

They's something kindo' harty-like about the atmusfere
When the heat of summer's over and the coolin' fall is here—
Of course we miss the flowers, and the blossums on the trees,
And the mumble of the hummin'birds and buzzin' of
    the bees;
But the air's so appetizin'; and the landscape through the haze
Of a crisp and sunny morning of the early autumn days
Is a pictur' that no painter has the colorin' to mock—
When the frost is on the punkin and the fodder's in the
    shock.

The husky, rusty russel of the tossels of the corn,
And the raspin' of the tangled leaves, as golden as the morn;
The stubble in the furries—kindo' lonesome-like, but still
A-preachin' sermuns to us of the barns they growed to fill;
The strawstack in the medder, and the reaper in the shed;
The hosses in theyr stalls below—the clover overhead!—
O, it sets my hart a-clickin' like the tickin' of a clock,
When the frost is on the punkin and the fodder's in
    the shock.

JAMES WHITCOMB RILEY

Rich Days

Welcome to you rich Autumn days,
   Ere comes the cold, leaf-picking wind,
When golden stooks are seen in fields,
   All standing arm-in-arm entwined;
And gallons of sweet cider seen
On trees in apples red and green.

With mellow pears that cheat our teeth,
   Which melt that tongues may suck them in;
With blue-black damsons, yellow plums,
   Now sweet and soft from stone to skin;
And woodnuts rich, to make us go
Into the loneliest lanes we know.

W. H. DAVIES

Autumn

The thistledown's flying, though the winds are all still,
On the green grass now lying, now mounting the hill,
The spring from the fountain now boils like a pot;
Through streams past the counting it bubbles red hot.

The ground parched and cracked is like overbaked bread,
The greensward all wracked is, bents dried up and dead.
The fallow fields glitter like water indeed,
And gossamers twitter, flung from weed unto weed.

Hilltops like hot iron glitter bright in the sun,
And the rivers we're eying burn to gold as they run;
Burning hot is the ground, liquid gold is the air;
Whoever looks round sees Eternity there.

JOHN CLARE

To Autumn

O Autumn, laden with fruit, and stained
With the blood of the grape, pass not, but sit
Beneath my shady roof; there thou mayest rest,
And tune thy jolly voice to my fresh pipe;

"The narrow bud opens her beauties to
The sun, and love runs in her thrilling veins;
Blossoms hang round the brows of morning, and
Flourish down the bright cheek of modest eve,
Till clust'ring Summer breaks forth into singing,
And feather'd clouds strew flowers round her
        head.

"The spirits of the air live on the smells
Of fruit; and joy, with pinions light, roves round
The gardens, or sits singing in the trees."
Thus sang the jolly Autumn as he sat;
Then rose, girded himself, and o'er the bleak
Hills fled from our sight; but left his golden load.

WILLIAM BLAKE

Real Property

Tell me about that harvest field.
Oh! Fifty acres of living bread.
The color has painted itself in my heart.
The form is patterned in my head.
So now I take it everywhere;
See it whenever I look round;
Hear it growing through every sound,
Know exactly the sound it makes—
Remembering, as one must all day,
Under the pavement the live earth aches.

Trees are at the farther end,
Limes all full of the mumbling bee;
So there must be a harvest field
Whenever one thinks of a linden tree.

A hedge is about it, very tall,
Hazy and cool, and breathing sweet.
Round paradise is such a wall
And all the day, in such a way,
In paradise the wild birds call.

You only need to close your eyes
And go within your secret mind,
And you'll be into paradise:
I've learnt quite easily to find
Some linden trees and drowsy bees,
A tall sweet hedge with the corn behind.

I will not have that harvest mown;
I'll keep the corn and leave the bread.
I've bought that field; it's now my own:
I've fifty acres in my head.
I take it as a dream to bed.
I carry it about all day. . . .

Sometimes when I have found a friend
I give a blade of corn away.

HAROLD MONRO

Apples in New Hampshire

Long poles support the branches of the orchards in New
     Hampshire,
Each bough fruited closely enough to take a prize;
The apple crop is heavy this year in New Hampshire:
Baldwins, McIntoshes, Winesaps, Northern Spies.
Hay is heaped in cocks on the sloping floors of the
     orchards,

So that none of the fruit may be lost in the tangled
    grasses.
Let the sun lie a few weeks more against the boughs of
    the orchards;
It will not be long before September passes.
The dew stands thickly beaded on the reddening cheeks
    of apples
When the sluggard autumn sun breaks through the mists;
Even when the moon shines, in the hard green apples
Ivory seeds blacken and ripening persists.
Sound core, wormy core, bruised and bitten,
The farmers' men will harvest them, heap after heap;
They will pick the best for market, they will shake the
    boughs and gather
Apples for cider, apples to keep.
Dark and cold in the earthy cellar,
Packed in barrels, laid upon shelves,
Filling the darkness with the redolence of summer,
Waiting for the children to help themselves,
White teeth piercing the glossy skins of apples—
The juice spurts and the cores are sweet and mellow;
There will be enough to last until March,
When the red skins wither and the pulp turns yellow.

And the bleak trees dreaming in the sharp still
    moonlight,
Snow nested in the crotches, rotted windfalls on the
    ground,
Will remember apples vaguely like a flood long
    remembered,
A mighty weight of apples, greedy and round,
Dragging their straining boughs lower and lower,
Sapping roots of their slow honey, stealing the dew.
The apple crop is heavy this year in New Hampshire;
Next year the trees will rest and apples will be few.

                                    MARIE GILCHRIST

A Day in Autumn

It will not always be like this,
The air windless, a few last
Leaves adding their decoration
To the trees' shoulders, braiding the cuffs
Of the boughs with gold; a bird preening
In the lawn's mirror. Having looked up
From the day's chores, pause a minute,
Let the mind take its photograph
Of the bright scene, something to wear
Against the heart in the long cold.

R. S. THOMAS

Pumpkins

At the end of the garden,
Across the litter of weeds and grass cuttings,
The pumpkin spreads its coarse,
Bristled, hollow-stemmed lines,
Erupting in great leaves
Above flowers
The nobbly and prominent
Stigmas of which
Are like fuses
Waiting to be set by bees.

When, like a string
Of yellow mines
Across the garden,
The pumpkins will smolder
And swell,
Drawing their combustion from the sun
To make their own.

At night I lie
Waiting for detonations,
Half expecting
To find the garden
Cratered like a moon.

JOHN COTTON

Cider Song

Jonathan,
Winesap,
Sheep-nose,
Pippin—
Tumbling from the branches,
Falling all around,
Hartford sweet,
Bellflower,
Baldwin,
Russet,
In an apple orgy
Rolling on the ground.

Maiden-blush,
Rambo,
Red cheek to amber,
Drunk with the autumn rain,
Tipsy with the sun,
Northern spy,
Greening,
Riotous and merry
Hoarders-up of summer,
Vintners every one.

Wonderful
To know
At the end of the harvest,
Apples in the orchard

Will be mellow
　　in a jug.
Wonderful
To know
In the white clutch of winter,
Apples in the orchard
Will be golden
In a mug.

Off to the press!
The wind is blowing colder,
Tumble in the hopper
As fast as you can.
Now there'll be
　　no need
For the faint heart to cower;
Apples in the orchard
Will be fire in a man!

MILDRED WESTON

Song

Again rejoicing Nature sees
　　Her robe assume its vernal hues;
Her leafy locks wave in the breeze,
　　All freshly steeped in morning dews.

In vain to me the cowslips blaw,
　　In vain to me the violets spring;
In vain to me in glen or shaw,
　　The mavis* and the lintwhite sing.

The merry plowboy cheers his team,
　　Wi' joy the tentie* seedsman stalks,
But life to me's a weary dream,
　　A dream of ane that never wauks.*

* mavis: *the song thrush;* tentie: *attentive;* wauks: *wakes*

The wanton coot the water skims,
    Amang the reeds the ducklings cry,
The stately swan majestic swims,
    And everything is blest but I.

The shepherd steeks* his faulding slap,*
    And owre the moorland whistles shrill;
Wi' wild, unequal, wand'ring step
    I meet him on the dewy hill.

And when the lark, 'tween light and dark,
    Blithe waukens by the daisy's side,
And mounts and sings on flittering wings,
    A woe-worn ghaist* I hameward glide.

Come, winter, with thine angry howl,
    And raging bend the naked tree;
Thy gloom will soothe my cheerless soul,
    When nature all is sad like me!

ROBERT BURNS

* steeks: *shuts;* slap: *gate;* ghaist: *ghost*

About the Woodlands
I Will Go

Trees and the Woods

Loveliest of Trees

Loveliest of trees, the cherry now
Is hung with bloom along the bough,
And stands about the woodland ride
Wearing white for Eastertide.

Now, of my threescore years and ten,
Twenty will not come again,
And take from seventy springs a score,
It only leaves me fifty more.

And since to look at things in bloom
Fifty springs are little room,
About the woodlands I will go
To see the cherry hung with snow.

A. E. HOUSMAN

Planting Trees

Today six slender fruit trees stand
Where yesterday were none;
They have been planted by my hand,
And they shall dazzle in the sun
When all my springs are done.

Two apples shall unfold their rose,
Two cherries their snow, two pears;
And fruit shall hang where blossom blows,
When I am gone from these sweet airs
To where none knows or cares.

My heart is glad, my heart is high
With sudden ecstasy;
I have given back, before I die,
Some thanks for every lovely tree
That dead men grew for me.

V. H. FRIEDLAENDER

The Trees Are Down

—and he cried with a loud voice:
Hurt not the earth, neither the sea, nor the trees—
(Revelation.)

They are cutting down the great plane trees at the end
of the gardens.
For days there has been the grate of the saw, the swish
of the branches as they fall,
The crash of trunks, the rustle of trodden leaves,
With the "Whoops" and the "Whoas," the loud common
talk, the loud common laughs of the men,
above it all.

I remember one evening of a long past Spring
Turning in at a gate, getting out of a cart, and finding
        a large dead rat in the mud of the drive.
I remember thinking: alive or dead, a rat was a god-
        forsaken thing,
But at least, in May, that even a rat should be alive.

The week's work here is as good as done. There is just
        one bough
  On the roped bole, in the fine gray rain,
    Green and high
    And lonely against the sky.
      (Down now!—)
    And but for that,
    If an old dead rat
Did once, for a moment, unmake the Spring, I might
        never have thought of him again.

It is not for a moment the Spring is unmade today;
These were great trees, it was in them from root to stem:
When the men with the "Whoops" and the "Whoas"
        have carted the whole of the whispering
        loveliness away
Half the Spring, for me, will have gone with them.

It is going now, and my heart has been struck with the
        hearts of the planes;
Half my life it has beat with these, in the sun, in the
        rains,
    In the March wind, the May breeze,
In the great gales that came over to them across the roofs
        from the great seas.
    There was only a quiet rain when they were
    dying;
    They must have heard the sparrows flying,
And the small creeping creatures in the earth where they
        were lying—
    But I, all day, I heard an angel crying:
    "Hurt not the trees."

CHARLOTTE MEW

Solitude

How still it is here in the woods. The trees
Stand motionless, as if they did not dare
To stir, lest it should break the spell. The air
Hangs quiet as spaces in a marble frieze.
Even this little brook, that runs at ease,
Whispering and gurgling in its knotted bed,
Seems but to deepen, with its curling thread
Of sound, the shadowy sun-pierced silences.
Sometimes a hawk screams or a woodpecker
Startles the stillness from its fixéd mood
With his loud careless tap. Sometimes I hear
The dreamy whitethroat from some far-off tree
Pipe slowly on the listening solitude,
His five pure notes succeeding pensively.

ARCHIBALD LAMPMAN

The Fallen Tree

The shade once swept about your boughs
Quietly obsequious
To the time-keeping sun;
Now, fallen tree, you with that shade are one.

From chalky earth as white as surf
Beneath the uptorn turf
Roots hang in empty space
Like snakes about the pale Medusa's face.

And as I perch on a forked branch,
More used to squirrel's haunch,
I think how dead you are,
More dead than upright post or fence or chair.

ANDREW YOUNG

Tree at My Window

Tree at my window, window tree,
My sash is lowered when night comes on;
But let there never be curtain drawn
Between you and me.

Vague dream-head lifted out of the ground,
And thing next most diffuse to cloud,
Not all your light tongues talking aloud
Could be profound.

But, tree, I have seen you taken and tossed,
And if you have seen me when I slept,
You have seen me when I was taken and swept
And all but lost.

That day she put our heads together,
Fate had her imagination about her,
Your head so much concerned with outer,
Mine with inner, weather.

ROBERT FROST

Leaves

Leaves of the summer, lovely summer's pride,
   Sweet is the shade below your silent tree,
Whether in waving copses, where ye hide
   My roamings, or in fields that let me see
   The open sky; and whether ye may be
Around the low-stemm'd oak, robust and wide;
Or taper ash upon the mountain side;
   Or lowland elm; your shade is sweet to me.

Whether ye wave above the early flow'rs
    In lively green; or whether, rustling sere,
Ye fly on playful winds, around my feet,

In dying autumn; lovely are your bow'rs,
    Ye early-dying children of the year;
        Holy the silence of your calm retreat.

WILLIAM BARNES

Tapestry Trees

Oak. I am the rooftree and the keel:
I bridge the seas for woe and weal.

Fir. High o'er the lordly oak I stand,
And drive him on from land to land.

Ash. I heft my brother's iron bane;
I shaft the spear and build the wain.

Yew. Dark down the windy dale I grow,
The father of the fateful bow.

Poplar. The war shaft and the milking bowl
I make, and keep the hay wain whole.

Olive. The King I bless; the lamps I trim;
In my warm wave do fishes swim.

Apple tree. I bowed my head to Adam's will;
The cups of toiling men I fill.

Pine. I draw the blood from out the earth:
I store the sun for winter mirth.

Orange tree. Amidst the greenness of my night
My odorous lamps hang round and bright.

Fig tree. I who am little among trees
In honey-making mate the bees.

Mulberry tree. Love's lack hath dyed my berries
    red:
For Love's attire my leaves are shed.

Pear tree. High o'er the mead flowers' hidden feet
I bear aloft my burden sweet.

Bay. Look on my leafy boughs, the Crown
Of living song and dead renown!

WILLIAM MORRIS

Stopping by Woods on a Snowy Evening

Whose woods these are I think I know.
His house is in the village though;
He will not see me stopping here
To watch his woods fill up with snow.

My little horse must think it queer
To stop without a farmhouse near
Between the woods and frozen lake
The darkest evening of the year.

He gives his harness bells a shake
To ask if there is some mistake.
The only other sound's the sweep
Of easy wind and downy flake.

The woods are lovely, dark and deep,
But I have promises to keep,
And miles to go before I sleep,
And miles to go before I sleep.

ROBERT FROST

A Young Birch

The birch begins to crack its outer sheath
Of baby green and show the white beneath,
As whosoever likes the young and slight
May well have noticed. Soon entirely white
To double day and cut in half the dark
It will stand forth, entirely white in bark,
And nothing but the top a leafy green—
The only native tree that dares to lean,
Relying on its beauty, to the air.
(Less brave perhaps than trusting are the fair.)
And someone reminiscent will recall
How once in cutting brush along the wall
He spared it from the number of the slain,
At first to be no bigger than a cane,
And then no bigger than a fishing pole,
But now at last so obvious a bole
The most efficient help you ever hired
Would know that it was there to be admired,
And zeal would not be thanked that cut it down
When you were reading books or out of town.
It was a thing of beauty and was sent
To live its life out as an ornament.

ROBERT FROST

The Beech

Strength leaves the hand I lay on this beech bole
    So great-girthed, old and high;
Its sprawling arms like iron serpents roll
    Between me and the sky.

One elbow on the sloping earth it leans,
    That steeply falls beneath,
As though resting a century it means
    To take a moment's breath.

Its long thin buds in glistering varnish dipt
    Are swinging up and down
While one young beech that winter left unstript
    Still wears its withered crown.

At least gust of the wind the great tree heaves
    From heavy twigs to groin;
The wind sighs as it rakes among dead leaves
    For some lost key or coin.

And my blood shivers as away it sweeps
    Rustling the leaves that cling
Too late to that young withered beech that keeps
    Its autumn in the spring.

ANDREW YOUNG

Binsey Poplars Felled 1879

My aspens dear, whose airy cages quelled,
Quelled or quenched in leaves the leaping sun,
All felled, felled, are all felled;
    Of a fresh and following folded rank

Not spared, not one
That dandled a sandaled
Shadow that swam or sank
On meadow and river and wind-wandering weed-winding
bank.

O if we but knew what we do
When we delve or hew—
Hack and rack the growing green!
Since country is so tender
To touch, her being só slender,
That, like this sleek and seeing ball
But a prick will make no eye at all,
Where we, even where we mean
To mend her we end her,
When we hew or delve:
Aftercomers cannot guess the beauty been.
Ten or twelve, only ten or twelve
Strokes of havoc únselve
The sweet especial scene,
Rural scene, a rural scene,
Sweet especial rural scene.

GERARD MANLEY HOPKINS

Unharvested

A scent of ripeness from over a wall.
And come to leave the routine road
And look for what had made me stall,
There sure enough was an apple tree
That had eased itself of its summer load,
And of all but its trivial foliage free,
Now breathed as light as a lady's fan.
For there there had been an apple fall
As complete as the apple had given man.
The ground was one circle of solid red.

May something go always unharvested!
May much stay out of our stated plan,
Apples or something forgotten and left,
So smelling their sweetness would be no theft.

ROBERT FROST

A Pastoral

The wise old apple tree in spring,
Though split and hollow, makes a crown
Of such fantastic blossoming
We cannot let them cut it down.
It bears no fruit, but honey bees
Prefer it to the other trees.

The orchard man chalks his mark
And says, "This empty shell must go."
We nod and rub it off the bark
As soon as he goes down the row.
Each spring he looks bewildered. "Queer,
I thought I marked this thing last year."

Ten orchard men have come and gone
Since first I saw my grandfather
Slyly erase it. I'm the one
To do it now. As I defer
The showy veteran's removal
My grandson nods his full approval.

Like mine, my fellow ancient's roots
Are deep in the last century
From which our memories send shoots
For all our grandchildren to see
How spring, inviting bloom and rhyme,
Defeats the orchard men of time.

ROBERT HILLYER

Under the Boughs

Prefer the cherry when the fruit hangs thick
and hot for plunder of a blackbird's beak,
the bird flashing and crying in the leaves.

Shadow and sun and blackbird in the leaves
make summer's ripeness, the blood's sweet, slow heat,
when there is this hot, red-fleshed fruit to eat.

I will not ask you to believe sweetness
of fruit beyond all possible sweetness
when the sugary juice stains lips and teeth.

I will not ask you to believe surfeit
is possible. The sun burns at your shut
eyelids; the sun warms at your shadowed cheek.

Only hear the birds crying in the leaves.
Long ago there were white-trembling blossoms
upon the boughs where full fruit hangs now.

GENE BARO

Peach Tree with Fruit

Amid curled leaves and green,
Globes that have glow and sheen!
Fruit most aerial,
Fruit rose-flushed and pale!

But molded on a stone—
It weights the bodies down
Where their bright flesh corrupts
Sooner than crabbèd fruits.

Peach! Most flower-like fruit!
Two seasons in one growth—
Autumn's glow and sheen
Amid the summer's green!

PADRAIC COLUM

Come In

As I came to the edge of the woods,
Thrush music—hark!
Now if it was dusk outside,
Inside it was dark.

Too dark in the woods for a bird
By sleight of wing
To better its perch for the night,
Though it still could sing.

The last of the light of the sun
That had died in the west
Still lived for one song more
In a thrush's breast.

Far in the pillared dark
Thrush music went—
Almost like a call to come in
To the dark and lament.

But no, I was out for stars:
I would not come in.
I meant not even if asked,
And I hadn't been.

ROBERT FROST

The Woodlands

O spread agen your leaves an' flow'rs,
    Luonesome woodlands! zunny woodlands!
Here undernëath the dewy show'rs
    O warm-âir'd springtime, zunny woodlands.
As when, in drong* ar oben groun',
Wi' happy buoyish heart I voun'
The twitt'ren birds a' builden roun'
    Your high-bough'd hedges, zunny woodlands.

Ya gie'd me life, ya gie'd me jày,
    Luonesome woodlands, zunny woodlands;
Ya gie'd me health as in my plây
    I rambled droo ye, zunny woodlands.
Ya gie'd me freedom var to rove
In âiry meäd, ar shiady grove;
Ya gie'd me smilen Fanny's love,
    The best of al ō't, zunny woodlands.

My vust shrill skylark whiver'd high,
    Luonesome woodlands, zunny woodlands,
To zing below your deep-blue sky
    An' white spring-clouds, O zunny woodlands,
An' boughs o' trees that oonce stood here,
Wer glossy green the happy year
That gie'd me oon I lov'd so dear
    An' now ha lost, O zunny woodlands.

O let me rove agen unspied,
    Luonesome woodlands, zunny woodlands,
Along your green-bough'd hedges' zide,
    As then I rambled, zunny woodlands.
An' wher the missèn trees oonce stood,
Ar tongues oonce rung among the wood,
My memory shal miake em good,
    Though you've a-lost em, zunny woodlands.

WILLIAM BARNES

*drong: *a narrow way*

Strange Tree

Away beyond the Jarboe house
    I saw a different kind of tree.
Its trunk was old and large and bent,
    And I could feel it look at me.

The road was going on and on
    Beyond, to reach some other place.
I saw a tree that looked at me,
    And yet it did not have a face.

It looked at me with all its limbs;
    It looked at me with all its bark.
The yellow wrinkles on its sides
    Were bent and dark.

And then I ran to get away,
    But when I stopped and turned to see,
The tree was bending to the side
    And leaning out to look at me.

ELIZABETH MADOX ROBERTS

Trees

To be a giant and keep quiet about it,
To stay in one's own place;
To stand for the constant presence of process
And always to seem the same;
To be steady as a rock and always trembling,
Having the hard appearance of death
With the soft, fluent nature of growth,
One's Being deceptively armored,
One's Becoming deceptively vulnerable;
To be so tough, and take the light so well,
Freely providing forbidden knowledge

Of so many things about heaven and earth
For which we should otherwise have no word—
Poems or people are rarely so lovely,
And even when they have great qualities
They tend to tell you rather than exemplify
What they believe themselves to be about,
While from the moving silence of trees,
Whether in storm or calm, in leaf and naked,
Night or day, we draw conclusions of our own,
Sustaining and unnoticed as our breath,
And perilous also—though there has never been
A critical tree—about the nature of things.

HOWARD NEMEROV

Staying Alive

Staying alive in the woods is a matter of calming down
At first and deciding whether to wait for rescue,
Trusting to others,
Or simply to start walking and walking in one direction
Till you come out—or something happens to stop you.
By far the safer choice
Is to settle down where you are, and try to make a living
Off the land, camping near water, away from shadows.
Eat no white berries;
Spit out all bitterness. Shooting at anything
Means hiking further and further every day
To hunt survivors;
It may be best to learn what you have to learn without
    a gun.
Not killing but watching birds and animals go
In and out of shelter
At will. Following their example, build for a whole
    season:
Facing across the wind in your lean-to,
You may feel wilder,
But nothing, not even you, will have to stay in hiding.

If you have no matches, a stick and a fire-bow
Will keep you warmer,
Or the crystal of your watch, filled with water, held up
   to the sun
Will do the same in time. In case of snow
Drifting toward winter,
Don't try to stay awake through the night, afraid of
   freezing—
The bottom of your mind knows all about zero;
It will turn you over
And shake you till you waken. If you have trouble
   sleeping
Even in the best of weather, jumping to follow
With eyes strained to their corners
The unidentifiable noises of the night and feeling
Bears and packs of wolves nuzzling your elbow,
Remember the trappers
Who treated them indifferently and were left alone.
If you hurt yourself, no one will comfort you
Or take your temperature,
So stumbling, wading, and climbing are as dangerous as
   flying.
But if you decide, at last, you must break through
In spite of all danger,
Think of yourself by time and not by distance, counting
Wherever you're going by how long it takes you;
No other measure
Will bring you safe to nightfall. Follow no streams: they
   run
Under the ground or fall into wilder country.
Remember the stars
And moss when your mind runs into circles. If it should
   rain
Or the fog should roll the horizon in around you,
Hold still for hours
Or days if you must, or weeks, for seeing is believing
In the wilderness. And if you find a pathway,
Wheel-rut, or fence-wire,
Retrace it left or right: someone knew where he was going

Once upon a time, and you can follow
Hopefully, somewhere,
Just in case. There may even come, on some uncanny
    evening,
A time when you're warm and dry, well fed, not thirsty,
Uninjured, without fear,
When nothing, either good or bad, is happening.
This is called staying alive. It's temporary.
What occurs after
Is doubtful. You must always be ready for something
    to come bursting
Through the far edge of a clearing, running toward you,
Grinning from ear to ear
And hoarse with welcome. Or something crossing and
    hovering
Overhead, as light as air, like a break in the sky,
Wondering what you are.
Here you are face to face with the problem of
    recognition.
Having no time to make smoke, too much to say,
You should have a mirror
With a tiny hole in the back for better aiming, for
    reflecting
Whatever disaster you can think of, to show
The way you suffer.
These body signals have universal meaning: If you are
    lying
Flat on your back with arms outstretched behind you.
You say you require
Emergency treatment; if you are standing erect and
    holding
Arms horizontal, you mean you are not ready;
If you hold them over
Your head, you want to be picked up. Three of anything
Is a sign of distress. Afterward, if you see
No ropes, no ladders,
No maps or messages falling, no searchlights or trails
    blazing,
Then, chances are, you should be prepared to burrow
Deep for a deep winter.

DAVID WAGONER

The Wind Stood Up and Gave a Shout

Wind, Rain, and Storm

The Wind

The wind stood up, and gave a shout;
He whistled on his fingers, and

Kicked the withered leaves about,
And thumped the branches with his hand,

And said he'd kill, and kill, and kill;
And so he will! And so he will!

JAMES STEPHENS

The Beggar Wind

In winter when the nights are long
The beggar wind goes crying,
And seeks above the shallow ponds
In midland pastures lying.
He whines above the dozing marsh
And through the orchard shivers,
He frets the leafless poplar row
And whimpers to the river.

O kindly waters, give, he cries,
A-cold and still imploring,
To warm me give your garnered heat
The summer heat you're storing.
And so he wheedles beggar-wise
As through the dark he shivers,
So takes their dole and leaves behind
The ice on lakes and rivers.

MARY AUSTIN

A Strong Wind

All day a strong wind blew
Across the green and brown from Kerry.
The leaves hurrying, two
By three, over the road, collected
In chattering groups. New berry
Dipped with old branch. Careful insects
Flew low behind their hedges.
Held back by her pretty petticoat,
Butterfly struggled. A bit of
Paper, on which a schoolgirl had written
"Maire loves Jimmy," jumped up
Into a tree. Tapping in haste,
The wind was telegraphing, hundreds
Of miles. All Ireland raced.

AUSTIN CLARKE

Hearing the Wind at Night

I heard the wind coming,
transferred from tree to tree.
I heard the leaves
swish, wishing to be free

to come with the wind, yet wanting to stay
with the boughs like sleeves.
The wind was a green ghost.
Possessed of tearing breath

the body of each tree
whined, a whipping post,
then straightened and resumed
its vegetable oath.

I heard the wind going,
and it went wild.
Somewhere the forest threw itself
into tantrum like a child.

I heard the trees tossing
in punishment or grief,
then sighing, and soughing,
soothing themselves to sleep.

MAY SWENSON

Mid-country Blow

All night and all day the wind roared in the trees,
Until I could think there were waves rolling high as my
    bedroom floor;
When I stood at the window, an elm bough swept to
    my knees;
The blue spruce lashed like a surf at the door.

The second dawn I would not have believed:
The oak stood with each leaf stiff as a bell.
When I looked at the altered scene, my eye was
    undeceived,
But my ear still kept the sound of the sea like a shell.

THEODORE ROETHKE

Signs of Rain

*Forty reasons for not accepting an invitation
of a friend to make an excursion with him*

1 The hollow winds begin to blow;
2 The clouds look black, the glass is low,
3 The soot falls down, the spaniels sleep,
4 And spiders from their cobwebs peep.
5 Last night the sun went pale to bed,
6 The moon in halos hid her head;
7 The boding shepherd heaves a sigh,
8 For see, a rainbow spans the sky!
9 The walls are damp, the ditches smell,
10 Closed is the pink-eyed pimpernel.
11 Hark how the chairs and tables crack!
12 Old Betty's nerves are on the rack;
13 Loud quacks the duck, the peacocks cry,
14 The distant hills are seeming nigh.
15 How restless are the snorting swine!
16 The busy flies disturb the kine,
17 Low o'er the grass the swallow wings,
18 The cricket, too, how sharp he sings!
19 Puss on the hearth, with velvet paws,
20 Sits wiping o'er her whiskered jaws;
21 Through the clear streams the fishes rise,
22 And nimbly catch the incautious flies.
23 The glowworms, numerous and light,
24 Illumed the dewy dell last night;
25 At dusk the squalid toad was seen,
26 Hopping and crawling o'er the green;
27 The whirling dust the wind obeys,
28 And in the rapid eddy plays;
29 The frog has changed his yellow vest
30 And in a russet coat is dressed.
31 Though June, the air is cold and still,

32 The mellow blackbird's voice is shrill;
33 My dog, so altered in his taste,
34 Quits mutton bones on grass to feast;
35 And see yon rooks, how odd their flight!
36 They imitate the gliding kite,
37 And seem precipitate to fall,
38 As if they felt the piercing ball.
39 'T will surely rain; I see with sorrow,
40 Our jaunt must be put off tomorrow.

EDWARD JENNER

Deluge

The maiden ran away to fetch the clothes
And threw her apron o'er her cap and bows;
But the shower catched her ere she hurried in
And beat and almost dowsed her to the skin.
The ruts ran brooks as they would ne'er be dry,
And the boy waded as he hurried by;
The half-drowned plowman waded to the knees,
And birds were almost drowned upon the trees.
The streets ran rivers till they floated o'er,
And women screamed to meet it at the door.
Labor fled home and rivers hurried by,
And still it fell as it would never stop;
E'en the old stone pit, deep as house is high,
Was brimming o'er and floated o'er the top.

JOHN CLARE

Rain

It ain't no use to grumble and complain;
    It's jest as cheap and easy to rejoice;
When God sorts out the weather and sends rain,
    Why, rain's my choice.

JAMES WHITCOMB RILEY

On a Wet Day

As I walk'd thinking through a little grove,
Some girls that gathered flowers came passing me,
Saying, "Look, here! look there!" delightedly.
"Oh, here it is!" "What's that?" "A lily, love."
"And there are violets!"
"Further for roses! Oh, the lovely pets—
The darling beauties! Oh, the nasty thorn!
Look here, my hand's all torn!"
"What's that that jumps!" "Oh, don't! it's a
        grasshopper!"
"Come run, come run,
Here's bluebells!" "Oh, what fun!"
"Not that way! Stop her!"
"Yes, this way!" "Pluck them, then!"
"Oh, I've found mushrooms! Oh, look here!" "Oh, I'm
Quite sure that further on we'll get wild thyme."

"Oh, we shall stay too long, it's going to rain!
There's lightning, oh there's thunder!"
"Oh, shan't we hear the vesper bell, I wonder?"
"Why, it's not nones, you silly little thing;
And don't you hear the nightingales that sing
Fly away O die away?"
"Oh, I hear something! Hush!"
"Why, where? what is it, then?" "Ah! in that bush!"
So every girl here knocks it, shakes and shocks it,
Till with the stir they make
Out scurries a great snake.
"O Lord! O me! Alack! Ah me! alack!"
They scream, and then all run and scream again,
And then in heavy drops down comes the rain.

Each running at the other in a fright,
Each trying to get before the other, and crying
And flying, stumbling, tumbling, wrong or right;

One sets her knee
There where her foot should be;
One has her hands and dress
All smothered up with mud in a fine mess;
And one gets trampled on by two or three.
What's gathered is let fall
About the wood and not picked up at all.
The wreaths of flowers are scattered on the ground;
And still screaming hustling without rest
They run this way and that and round and round,
She thinks herself in luck who runs the best.

I stood quite still to have a perfect view,
And never noticed till I got wet through.

FRANCO SACCHETTI
Translated by Dante Gabriel Rossetti

And Then It Rained

And then it rained, oh, then it rained,
All night, all day, it rained and rained.
And the birds stayed home
And brooded their young.
And the waterfall, roaring,
Was brown with mud.

And then it stopped, oh, then it stopped.
Sun broke through, and the raining stopped.
And the birds came forth
And sang on the posts.
And the waterfall, thinning,
Was bright as glass.

MARK VAN DOREN

Moods of Rain

It can be so tedious, a bore
Telling a long dull story you have heard before
So often it is meaningless;
Yet, in another mood,
It comes swashbuckling, swishing a million foils,
Feinting at daffodils, peppering tin pails,
Pelting so fast on roof, umbrella, hood,
You hear long silk being torn;
Refurbishes old toys and oils
Slick surfaces that gleam as if unworn.
Sometimes a cordial summer rain will fall
And string on railings delicate small bells;
Soundless as seeds on soil
Make green ghosts rise.
And it can be fierce, hissing like blazing thorns,
Or side-drums hammering at night-filled eyes
Until you wake and hear a long grief boil
And, overflowing, sluice
The lost raft of the world.
Yet it can come as lenitive and calm
As comfort from the mother of us all
Sighing you into sleep
Where peace prevails and only soft rains fall.

VERNON SCANNELL

A Thunder-storm

The wind began to rock the grass
With threatening tunes and low—
He flung a menace at the earth,
A menace at the sky.

The leaves unhooked themselves from trees
And started all abroad;
The dust did scoop itself like hands
And throw away the road.

The wagons quickened on the streets,
The thunder hurried slow;
The lightning showed a yellow beak,
And then a livid claw.

The birds put up the bars to nests,
The cattle fled to barns;
There came one drop of giant rain,
And then, as if the hands

That held the dam had parted hold,
The waters wrecked the sky,
But overlooked my father's house
Just quartering a tree.

EMILY DICKINSON

The Rhyme of the Rain Machine

Said Jeremy Jonathan Joseph Jones
    "The weather is far too dry,
So I reckon I'll have to stir my bones
And try the effect of concussive tones
    Upon the lazy sky."

So Jeremy Jonathan Joseph went
    Away to the nearest town:
And there his money was quickly spent
For queer contraptions all intent
    To make the rain come down.

There were cannon, and mortars, and lots of
    shells,
    And dynamite by the ton;
With a gas balloon and a chime of bells
And various other mystic spells
    To overcloud the sun.

The day was fair and the sky was bright,
    And never a cloud was seen;
When Jeremy Jonathan set alight
His biggest fuse and screwed up tight
    The joints of the rain machine.

He fired a shot, and barely two,
    When the sky began to pale;
The third one brought a heavy dew,
But at the fourth tornadoes blew,
    With thunder, rain, and hail.

It rained all night and another day,
    And then for a week or more;
It flooded the farm in a scandalous way,
And drowned poor Jeremy, sad to say,
    Who couldn't stop the pour.

O! Jeremy Jonathan Joseph Jones,
    Your farm was fair to see;
But now a lake lies over its stones,
From whose dark bosom horrific moans
    Are heard nocturnallee.

To check the flood you started, I've heard
    All efforts were in vain;
Until the Bureau at Washington stirred,
And stopped the storm with a single word,
    By just predicting—Rain!

                  F. W. CLARKE

The Shower

Waters above! Eternal springs!
The dew that silvers the dove's wings!
O welcome, welcome to the sad:
Give dry dust drink, drink that makes glad!
Many fair ev'nings, many flow'rs
Sweetened with rich and gentle showers,
Have I enjoyed, and down have run
Many a fine and shining sun;
But never, till this happy hour,
Was blest with such an evening shower!

HENRY VAUGHAN

Thunder

Call the cows home!
Call the cows home!
Louring storm clouds
Hitherward come;
East to West
Their wings are spread;
Lost in the blue
Is each heaven-high head;
They've dimmed the sun;
Turned day to night;
With a whistling wind
The woods are white;
Down streams the rain
On farm, barn, byre,
Bright green hill,
And bramble and brier,
Filling the valley
With glimmer and gloom:
Call the cows home!
Call the cows home!

WALTER DE LA MARE

Giant Thunder

Giant Thunder, striding home,
Wonders if his supper's done.

"Hag wife, hag wife, bring me bones!"
"They are not done," the old hag moans.

"Not done? not done?" the giant roars,
And heaves the old wife out of doors.

Cries he, "I'll have them, cooked or not!"
And overturns the cooking pot.

He flings the burning coals about;
See how the lightning flashes out!

Upon the gale the old hag rides,
The clouded moon for terror hides.

All the world with thunder quakes;
Forest shudders, mountain shakes;

From the cloud the rainstorm breaks;
Village ponds are turned to lakes;
Every living creature wakes.

Hungry giant, lie you still!
Stamp no more from hill to hill—
Tomorrow you shall have your fill.

JAMES REEVES

The Storm

We wake to hear the storm come down,
    Sudden on roof and pane;
The thunder's loud and the hasty wind
    Hurries the beating rain.

The rain slackens, the wind blows gently,
    The gust grows gentle and stills,
And the thunder, like a breaking stick,
    Stumbles about the hills.

The drops still hang on leaf and thorn,
    The downs stand up more green;
The sun comes out again in power
    And the sky is washed and clean.

EDWARD SHANKS

Hatteras Calling

Southeast, and storm, and every weathervane
shivers and moans upon its dripping pin,
ragged on chimneys the cloud whips, the rain
howls at the flues and windows to get in,

the golden rooster claps his golden wings
and from the Baptist Chapel shrieks no more,
the golden arrow into the southeast sings
and hears on the roof the Atlantic Ocean roar.

Waves among wires, sea scudding over poles,
down every alley the magnificence of rain,
dead gutters live once more, the deep manholes
hollo in triumph a passage to the main.

Umbrellas, and in the Gardens one old man
hurries away along a dancing path,
listens to music on a watering-can,
observes among the tulips the sudden wrath,

pale willows thrashing to the needled lake,
and dinghies filled with water; while the sky
smashes the lilacs, swoops to shake and break,
till shattered branches shriek and railings cry.

Speak, Hatteras, your language of the sea:
scour with kelp and spindrift the stale street:
that man in terror may learn once more to be
child of that hour when rock and ocean meet.

CONRAD AIKEN

When Icicles Hang by the Wall

Snow and Winter

Winter

When icicles hang by the wall
    And Dick the shepherd blows his nail,
And Tom bears logs into the hall,
    And milk comes frozen home in pail;
When blood is nipt, and ways be foul,
Then nightly sings the staring owl
      Tu-whoo!
Tu-whit, tu-whoo! A merry note!
While greasy Joan doth keel the pot.

When all about the wind doth blow,
    And coughing drowns the parson's saw,
And birds sit brooding in the snow,
    And Marion's nose looks red and raw:
When roasted crabs hiss in the bowl—
Then nightly sings the staring owl
      Tu-whoo!
Tu-whit, tu-whoo! A merry note!
While greasy Joan doth keel the pot.

WILLIAM SHAKESPEARE

In Winter

It is hard, inland,
    in winter,
when the fields are motionless in snow,

to remember waves, to remember
    the wide, sloshing
immensity

of the Atlantic, continuous,
    green in the cold, taking snow
or rain into itself,

to realize the endurance
    of the tilting bell buoy
(hour by hour, years

through) that clangs, clangs,
    leaning
with the rocking waters, miles

from land; even in storm and
    night-howling
snow, wet, red, flashing

to mark the channel. Some
    things
are, even if no one comes.

ROBERT WALLACE

Beclouded

The sky is low, the clouds are mean,
A traveling flake of snow
Across a barn or through a rut
Debates if it will go.

A narrow wind complains all day
How some one treated him;
Nature, like us, is sometimes caught
Without her diadem.

EMILY DICKINSON

Hard Frost

Frost called to water "Halt!"
And crusted the moist snow with sparkling salt.
Brooks, their own bridges, stop,
And icicles in long stalactites drop,
And tench in water holes
Lurk under gluey glass like fish in bowls.

In the hard-rutted lane
At every footstep breaks a brittle pane,
And tinkling trees ice-bound,
Changed into weeping willows, sweep the ground;
Dead boughs take root in ponds
And ferns on windows shoot their ghostly fronds.

But vainly the fierce frost
Interns poor fish, ranks trees in an armed host,
Hangs daggers from house eaves
And on the windows ferny ambush weaves;
In the long war grown warmer
The sun will strike him dead and strip his armor.

ANDREW YOUNG

Winter Portrait

A wrinkled, crabbed man they picture thee,
Old Winter, with a rugged beard as gray
As the long moss upon the apple tree;
Blue lipped, an ice drop at thy sharp blue nose,
Close muffled up, and on thy dreary way
Plodding alone through sleet and drifting snows.
They should have drawn thee by the high-leaped hearth,
Old Winter! seated in thy great armed chair,
Watching the children at their Christmas mirth.

ROBERT SOUTHEY

Ice

When Winter scourged the meadow and the hill
And in the withered leafage worked his will,
The water shrank, and shuddered, and stood still,—
Then built himself a magic house of glass,
Irised with memories of flowers and grass,
Wherein to sit and watch the fury pass.

CHARLES G. D. ROBERTS

Winter Rain

Every valley drinks,
      Every dell and hollow:
Where the kind rain sinks and sinks,
      Green of Spring will follow.

Yet a lapse of weeks
      Buds will burst their edges,
Strip their wool-coats, glue-coats, streaks,
      In the woods and hedges;

Weave a bower of love
    For birds to meet each other,
Weave a canopy above
    Nest and egg and mother.

But for fattening rain
    We should have no flowers,
Never a bud or leaf again
    But for soaking showers;

Never a mated bird
    In the rocking treetops,
Never indeed a flock or herd
    To graze upon the lea-crops.

Lambs so woolly white,
    Sheep the sun-bright leas on,
They could have no grass to bite
    But for rain in season.

We should find no moss
    In the shadiest places,
Find no waving meadow grass
    Pied with broad-eyed daisies:

But miles of barren sand,
    With never a son or daughter,
Not a lily on the land,
    Or lily on the water.

CHRISTINA ROSSETTI

Frost

What swords and spears, what daggers bright
He arms the morning with! How light
His powder is, that's fit to lie
On the wings of a butterfly!

What milk-white clothing he has made
For every little twig and blade!
What curious silver work is shown
On wood and iron, glass and stone!
"If you, my slim Jack Frost, can trace
This work so fine, so full of grace,
Tell me," I said, "before I go—
Where is your plump young sister, Snow?"

W. H. DAVIES

The Winter Lakes

Out in a world of death, far to the northward lying,
Under the sun and the moon, under the dusk and
the day;
Under the glimmer of stars and the purple of sunsets
dying,
Wan and waste and white, stretch the great lakes away.

Never a bud of spring, never a laugh of summer,
Never a dream of love, never a song of bird;
But only the silence and white, the shores that grow
chiller and dumber,
Wherever the ice-winds sob, and the griefs of winter
are heard.

Crags that are black and wet out of the gray lake
looming,
Under the sunset's flush, and the pallid, faint
glimmer of dawn;
Shadowy, ghostlike shores, where midnight surfs are
booming
Thunders of wintry woe over the spaces wan.

Lands that loom like specters, whited regions of winter,
Wastes of desolate woods, deserts of water and shore;

A world of winter and death, within these regions who enter,
    Lost to summer and life, go to return no more.

Moons that glimmer above, waters that lie white under,
    Miles and miles of lake far out under the night;
Foaming crests of waves, surfs that shoreward thunder,
    Shadowy shapes that flee, haunting the spaces white.

Lonely hidden bays, moon-lit, ice-rimmed, winding,
    Fringed by forests and crags, haunted by shadowy
        shores;
Hushed from the outward strife, where the mighty surf
      is grinding
Death and hate on the rocks, as sandward and
      landward it roars.

WILFRED CAMPBELL

A Warm Winter Day

    The mist condenses.
    The foliage drips
    And drips

    High in the tree
    Next to the Chinese pine
    Two peacocks sit;
    Their tail feathers hanging
    Bedraggled

    The fountain is unfreezing.
    Below the cracked ice-lumps
    Goldfish wait.

    Seed pods wait
    With their sealed orders.

JULIAN COOPER

The Death of the Flowers

The melancholy days are come, the saddest of the year,
Of wailing winds, and naked woods, and meadows brown
and sear.
Heaped in the hollows of the grove, the withered leaves
lie dead:
They rustle to the eddying gust, and to the rabbit's
tread.
The robin and the wren are flown, and from the shrubs
the jay,
And from the wood-top calls the crow, through all the
gloomy day.

Where are the flowers, the fair young flowers, that lately
sprang and stood
In brighter light and softer airs, a beauteous sisterhood?
Alas! they all are in their graves, the gentle race of
flowers
Are lying in their lowly beds, with the fair and good of
ours.
The rain is falling where they lie, but the cold November
rain
Calls not, from out the gloomy earth, the lovely ones
again.

The windflower and the violet, they perished long ago,
And the brier rose and the orchis died amid the summer
glow;
But on the hill the goldenrod, and the aster in the wood,
And the yellow sunflower by the brook in autumn beauty
stood,
Till fell the frost from the clear cold heaven, as falls the
plague on men,
And the brightness of their smile was gone, from upland,
glade, and glen.

And now, when comes the calm mild day, as still such
    days will come,
To call the squirrel and the bee from out their winter
    home;
When the sound of dropping nuts is heard, though all
    the trees are still,
And twinkle in the smoky light the waters of the rill,
The south wind searches for the flowers whose fragrance
    late he bore,
And sighs to find them in the wood and by the stream
    no more.

And then I think of one who in her youthful beauty
    died,
The fair, meek blossom that grew up and faded by my
    side;
In the cold moist earth we laid her, when the forest cast
    the leaf,
And we wept that one so lovely should have a life so
    brief:
Yet not unmeet it was that one, like that young friend
    of ours,
So gentle and so beautiful, should perish with the flowers.

WILLIAM CULLEN BRYANT

from Improvisations: Light and Snow

When I was a boy, and saw bright rows of icicles
In many lengths along a wall
I was disappointed to find
That I could not play music upon them:
I ran my hand lightly across them
And they fell, tinkling.
I tell you this, young man, so that your expectations of life
Will not be too great.

CONRAD AIKEN

Winter in the Fens

So moping flat and low our valleys lie,
So dull and muggy is our winter sky,
Drizzling from day to day with threats of rain,
And when that falls still threatening on again;
From one wet week so great an ocean flows
That every village to an island grows,
And every road for even weeks to come
Is stopt, and none but horsemen go from home;
And one wet night leaves travel's best in doubt,
And horseback travelers ask if floods are out
Of every passer-by, and with their horse
The meadow's ocean try in vain to cross;
The horse's footings with a sucking sound
Fill up with water on the firmest ground,
And ruts that dribble into brooks elsewhere
Can find no fall or flat to dribble here;
But filled with wet they brim and overflow
Till hollows in the road to rivers grow;
Then wind with sudden rage, abrupt and blea,
Twirls every lingering leaf from off each tree.
Such is our lowland scene that winter gives,
And strangers wonder where our comfort lives;
Yet in a little close, however keen
The winter comes, I find a patch of green,
Where robins, by the miser winter made
Domestic, flirt and perch upon the spade;
And in a little garden-close at home
I watch for spring—and there's the crocus come!

JOHN CLARE

Snow Harvest

The moon that now and then last night
Glanced between clouds in flight
Saw the white harvest that spread over
The stubble fields and even roots and clover.

It climbed the hedges, overflowed
And trespassed on the road,
Weighed down fruit trees and when winds woke
From white-thatched roofs rose in a silver smoke.

How busy is the world today!
Sun reaps, rills bear away
The lovely harvest of the snow
While bushes weep loud tears to see it go.

ANDREW YOUNG

To a Snowflake

What heart could have thought you?—
Past our devisal
(O filigree petal!)
Fashioned so purely,
Fragilely, surely,
From what Paradisal
Imagineless metal,
Too costly for cost?
Who hammered you, wrought you,
From argentine vapor?—
"God was my shaper.
Passing surmisal,
He hammered, He wrought me,
From curled silver vapor,
To lust of His mind:—

Thou couldst not have thought me!
So purely, so palely,
Tinily, surely,
Mightily, frailly,
Insculped and embossed,
With His hammer of wind,
And His graver of frost."

FRANCIS THOMPSON

First Sight

Lambs that learn to walk in snow
When their bleating clouds the air
Meet a vast unwelcome, know
Nothing but a sunless glare.
Newly stumbling to and fro
All they find, outside the fold,
Is a wretched width of cold.

As they wait beside the ewe,
Her fleeces wetly caked, there lies
Hidden round them, waiting too,
Earth's immeasurable surprise.
They could not grasp it if they knew,
What so soon will wake and grow
Utterly unlike the snow.

PHILIP LARKIN

Snow in the Suburbs

Every branch big with it,
Bent every twig with it;
Every fork like a white web-foot;
Every street and pavement mute:

Some flakes have lost their way, and grope back
    upward, when
Meeting those meandering down they turn and
    descend again.
    The palings are glued together like a wall,
    And there is no waft of wind with the fleecy
    fall.

    A sparrow enters the tree,
    Whereon immediately
A snow lump thrice his own slight size
Descends on him and showers his head and
    eyes,
    And overturns him,
    And near inurns him,
And lights on a nether twig, when its brush
Stars off a volley of other lodging lumps with a
    rush.

    The steps are a blanched slope,
    Up which, with feeble hope,
A black cat comes, wide eyed and thin;
    And we take him in.

THOMAS HARDY

Rhyming Riddle

I come more softly than a bird,
And lovely as a flower;
I sometimes last from year to year
And sometimes but an hour.
I stop the swiftest railroad train
Or break the stoutest tree.
And yet I am afraid of fire
And children play with me.

MARY AUSTIN

The Snowstorm

Announced by all the trumpets of the sky,
Arrives the snow, and, driving o'er the fields,
Seems nowhere to alight: the whited air
Hides hills and woods, the river, and the heaven,
And veils the farmhouse at the garden's end,
The sled and traveler stopped, the courier's feet
Delayed, all friends shut out, the housemates sit
Around the radiant fireplace, enclosed
In a tumultuous privacy of storm.

Come, see the north wind's masonry.
Out of an unseen quarry evermore
Furnished with tile, the fierce artificer
Curves his white bastions with projected roof
Round every windward stake or tree or door.
Speeding, the myriad-handed, his wild work
So fanciful, so savage, naught cares he
For number or proportion. Mockingly
On coop or kennel he hangs Parian wreaths;
A swanlike form invests the hidden thorn;
Fills up the farmer's lane from wall to wall,
Maugre the farmer's sighs; and at the gate
A tapering turret overtops the work.
And when his hours are numbered, and the world
Is all his own, retiring, as he were not.
Leaves, when the sun appears, astonished Art
To mimic in slow structures, stone by stone,
Built in an age, the mad wind's night-work,
The frolic architecture of the snow.

RALPH WALDO EMERSON

London Snow

When men were all asleep the snow came flying,
In large white flakes falling on the city brown,
Stealthily and perpetually settling and loosely lying,
　　Hushing the latest traffic of the drowsy town;
Deadening, muffling, stifling its murmurs failing;
Lazily and incessantly floating down and down:
　　Silently sifting and veiling road, roof and railing;
Hiding difference, making unevenness even,
Into angles and crevices softly drifting and sailing.
　　All night it fell, and when full inches seven
It lay in the depth of its uncompacted lightness,
The clouds blew off from a high and frosty heaven;
　　And all woke earlier for the unaccustomed brightness
Of the winter dawning, the strange unheavenly glare:
The eye marveled—marveled at the dazzling whiteness;
　　The ear hearkened to the stillness of the solemn air;
No sound of wheel rumbling nor of foot falling,
And the busy morning cries came thin and spare.
　　Then boys I heard, as they went to school, calling,
They gathered up the crystal manna to freeze
Their tongues with tasting, their hands with snowballing;
　　Or rioted in a drift, plunging up to the knees;
Or peering up from under the white-mossed wonder,
"O look at the trees!" they cried, "O look at the trees!"
　　With lessened load a few carts creak and blunder,
Following along the white deserted way,
A country company long dispersed asunder:
　　When now already the sun, in pale display
Standing by Paul's high dome, spread forth below
His sparkling beams, and awoke the stir of the day.
　　For now doors open, and war is waged with the snow;
And trains of somber men, past tale of number,
Tread long brown paths, as toward their toil they go:
　　But even for them awhile no cares encumber
Their minds diverted; the daily word is unspoken,

The daily thoughts of labor and sorrow slumber
At the sight of the beauty that greets them, for the
    charm they have broken.

ROBERT BRIDGES

Winter Morning

All night the wind swept over the house
And through our dream,
Swirling the snow up through the pines,
Ruffling the white, ice-capped clapboards,
Rattling the windows,
Rustling around and below our bed
So that we rode
Over wild water
In a white ship breasting the waves.
We rode through the night
On green, marbled
Water, and, half-waking, watched
The white, eroded peaks of icebergs
Sail past our windows;
Rode out the night in that north country,
And awoke, the house buried in snow,
Perched on a
Chill promontory, a
Giant's tooth
In the mouth of the cold valley,
Its white tongue looped frozen around us,
The trunks of tall birches
Revealing the rib cage of a whale
Stranded by a still stream;
And saw, through the motionless baleen of their
    branches,
As if through time,
Light that shone
On a landscape of ivory,
A harbor of bone.

WILLIAM JAY SMITH

Snowstorm

I

What a night! The wind howls, hisses, and but
    stops
To howl more loud, while the snow volley keeps
Incessant batter at the window pane,
Making our comforts feel as sweet again;
And in the morning, when the tempest drops,
At every cottage door mountainous heaps
Of snow lie drifted, that all entrance stops
Until the besom* and the shovel gain
The path, and leave a wall on either side.
The shepherd, rambling valleys white and wide,
With new sensations his old memory fills,
When hedges left at night, no more descried,
Are turned to one white sweep of curving hills,
And trees turned bushes half their bodies hide.

II

The boy that goes to fodder with surprise
Walks o'er the gate he opened yesternight.
The hedges all have vanished from his eyes;
E'en some treetops the sheep could reach to bite.
The novel scene engenders new delight,
And, though with cautious steps his sports begin,
He bolder shuffles the huge hills of snow,
Till down he drops and plunges to the chin,
And struggles much and oft escape to win—
Then turns and laughs but dare not further go;
For deep the grass and bushes lie below,
Where little birds that soon at eve went in
With heads tucked in their wings now pine for day
And little feel boys o'er their heads can stray.

JOHN CLARE

* besom: *broom*

White Fields

I

In the winter time we go
Walking in the fields of snow;

Where there is no grass at all;
Where the top of every wall,

Every fence, and every tree,
Is as white as white can be.

II

Pointing out the way we came,
—Every one of them the same—

All across the fields there be
Prints in silver filigree;

And our mothers always know,
By the footprints in the snow,

Where it is the children go.

JAMES STEPHENS

Work Without Hope

(Lines composed 21st February 1827)

All Nature seems at work. Slugs leave their lair—
The bees are stirring—birds are on the wing—
And Winter, slumbering in the open air,
Wears on his smiling face a dream of Spring!
And I the while, the sole unbusy thing,
Nor honey make, nor pair, nor build, nor sing.

Yet well I ken the banks where amaranths blow,
Have traced the fount whence streams of nectar flow.
Bloom, O ye amaranths! bloom for whom ye may,
For me ye bloom not! Glide, rich streams, away!
With lips unbrightened, wreathless brow, I stroll:
And would you learn the spells that drown my soul?
Work without Hope draws nectar in a sieve,
And Hope without an object cannot live.

SAMUEL TAYLOR COLERIDGE

Human Things

When the suns gets low, in winter,
The lapstreaked side of a red barn
Can put so flat a stop to its light
You'd think everything was finished.

Each dent, fray, scratch, or splinter,
Any gray weathering where the paint
Has scaled off, is a healed scar
Grown harder with the wounds of light.

Only a tree's trembling shadow
Crosses that ruined composure; even
Nail holes look deep enough to swallow
Whatever light has left to give.

And after sundown, when the wall
Slowly surrenders its color, the rest
Remains, its high, obstinate
Hulk more shadowy than the night.

HOWARD NEMEROV

Signs of Winter

The cat runs races with her tail. The dog
Leaps o'er the orchard hedge and gnarls the
    grass.
The swine run round and grunt and play with
    straw,
Snatching out hasty mouthfuls from the stack.
Sudden upon the elm-tree tops the crow
Unceremonious visit pays and croaks,
Then swoops away. From mossy barn the owl
Bobs hasty out—wheels round and, scared as soon,
As hastily retires. The ducks grow wild
And from the muddy pond fly up and wheel
A circle round the village and soon, tired,
Plunge in the pond again. The maids in haste
Snatch from the orchard hedge the mizzled clothes
And laughing hurry in to keep them dry.

                                    JOHN CLARE

Driving to Town Late to Mail a Letter

It is a cold and snowy night. The main street is deserted.
The only things moving are swirls of snow.
As I lift the mailbox door, I feel its cold iron.
There is a privacy I love in this snowy night.
Driving around, I will waste more time.

                                    ROBERT BLY

Nocturne

Over New England now, the snow
glitters on spruce and applewood;
the white owl hunts by dusk where late
the rabbits found the autumn good.

In Pennsylvania, the tall
farmer brings in his final hay,
the second growth; his oxen plod
under the last cold green of day.

In Delaware, the stacks of corn
march like brown tepees on the sky.
In Maryland, by Havre de Grace,
the fishers spread their nets to dry.

Deep in Virginia, the blue
piled mountains hide the westward path,
and rivers hunting for the sea
are red as the sundown's aftermath.

The silver onslaught of the tide
assails the Carolina coast,
where the full boughs of sounding oaks
defy the faint approach of frost.

In Georgia, darkness grows along
the wandering pine-straw roads; the sweet
fragrance of landward wind lies down
with the small bright blades of winter wheat.

In Florida, hibiscus clench
their scarlet blooms beneath the stars,
while the sun-warmed beaches and the sea
thunder their slow, eternal wars.

FRANCES FROST

To Stand and Stare

Various Celebrations of Nature's Miracles

Leisure

What is this life if, full of care,
We have no time to stand and stare?

No time to stand beneath the boughs
And stare as long as sheep or cows.

No time to see, when woods we pass,
Where squirrels hide their nuts in grass.

No time to see, in broad daylight,
Streams full of stars, like skies at night.

No time to turn at beauty's glance,
And watch her feet, how they can dance.

No time to wait till her mouth can
Enrich that smile her eyes began.

A poor life this if, full of care,
We have no time to stand and stare.

W. H. DAVIES

Farm Child

Look at this village boy, his head is stuffed
With all the nests he knows, his pockets with flowers,
Snail shells and bits of glass, the fruit of hours
Spent in the fields by thorn and thistle tuft.
Look at his eyes, see the harebell hiding there;
Mark how the sun has freckled his smooth face
Like a finch's egg under that bush of hair
That dares the wind, and in the mixen now
Notice his poise; from such unconscious grace
Earth breeds and beckons to the stubborn plow.

R. S. THOMAS

Under the Greenwood Tree

Under the greenwood tree
Who loves to lie with me,
And tune his merry note
Unto the sweet bird's throat—
Come hither, come hither, come hither!
    Here shall we see
    No enemy
But winter and rough weather.

Who doth ambition shun
And loves to live i' the sun,
Seeking the food he eats
And pleased with what he gets—
Come hither, come hither, come hither!
    Here shall he see
    No enemy
But winter and rough weather.

WILLIAM SHAKESPEARE

Prelude

Still south I went and west and south again,
Through Wicklow from the morning till the
    night,
And far from cities, and the sights of men,
Lived with the sunshine, and the moon's delight.

I knew the stars, the flowers, and the birds,
The gray and wintry sides of many glens,
And did but half remember human words,
In converse with the mountains, moors, and fens.

J. M. SYNGE

Immalee

I gather thyme upon the sunny hills,
    And its pure fragrance ever gladdens me,
    And in my mind having tranquillity
I smile to see how my green basket fills.
And by clear streams I gather daffodils;
    And in dim woods find out the cherry tree,
    And take its fruit and the wild strawberry
And nuts and honey; and live free from ills.
I dwell on the green earth, 'neath the blue sky,
    Birds are my friends, and leaves my rustling
        roof:
The deer are not afraid of me, and I
    Hear the wild goat, and hail its hastening
        hoof;
The squirrels sit perked as I pass them by,
    And even the watchful hare stands not aloof.

CHRISTINA ROSSETTI

In the Fields

Lord, when I look at lovely things which pass,
    Under old trees the shadow of young leaves
Dancing to please the wind along the grass,
    Or the gold stillness of the August sun on the August
        sheaves;
Can I believe there is a heavenlier world than this?
    And if there is
Will the strange heart of any everlasting thing
    Bring me these dreams that take my breath away?
They come at evening with the home-flying rooks and
        the scent of hay,
    Over the fields. They come in Spring.

CHARLOTTE MEW

Day of These Days

Such a morning it is when love
leans through geranium windows
and calls with a cockerel's tongue.

When red-haired girls scamper like roses
over the rain-green grass,
and the sun drips honey.

When hedgerows grow venerable,
berries dry black as blood,
and holes suck in their bees.

Such a morning it is when mice
run whispering from the church,
dragging dropped ears of harvest.

When the partridge draws back his spring
and shoots like a buzzing arrow
over grained and mahogany fields.

When no table is bare,
and no breast dry,
and the tramp feeds of ribs of rabbit.

Such a day it is when time
piles up the hills like pumpkins,
and the streams run golden.

When all men smell good,
and the cheeks of girls
are as baked bread to the mouth.

As bread and beanflowers
the touch of their lips,
and their white teeth sweeter than cucumbers.

LAURIE LEE

Planting Flowers on the Eastern Embankment

Written when Governor of Chung-Chou

I took money and bought flowering trees
And planted them out on the bank to the east of the keep.
I simply bought whatever had most blooms,
Not caring whether peach, apricot, or plum.
A hundred fruits, all mixed up together;
A thousand branches, flowering in due rotation.
Each has its season coming early or late;
But to all alike the fertile soil is kind.
The red flowers hang like a heavy mist;
The white flowers gleam like a fall of snow.
The wandering bees cannot bear to leave them;
The sweet birds also come there to roost.

In front there flows an ever-running stream;
Beneath there is built a little flat terrace.
Sometimes I sweep the flagstones of the terrace;
Sometimes, in the wind, I raise my cup and drink.
The flower branches screen my head from the sun;
The flower buds fall down into my lap.
Alone drinking, alone singing my songs
I do not notice that the moon is level with the steps.
The people of Pa do not care for flowers;
All the spring no one has come to look.
But their Governor General, alone with his cup of wine
Sits till evening and will not move from the place!

PO CHU-I (A.D. 772–846)

Translated from the Chinese by Arthur Waley

Afterwards

When the Present has latched its postern behind my
    tremulous stay,
    And the May month flaps its glad green leaves like
      wings,
Delicate-filmed as new-spun silk, will the neighbors say,
    "He was a man who used to notice such things"?

If it be in the dusk when, like an eyelid's soundless blink,
    The dewfall-hawk comes crossing the shades to alight
Upon the wind-warped upland thorn, a gazer may think,
    "To him this must have been a familiar sight."

If I pass during some nocturnal blackness, mothy and
    warm,
    When the hedgehog travels furtively over the lawn,
One may say, "He strove that such innocent creatures
    should come to no harm.
    But he could do little for them; and now he is gone."

If, when hearing that I have been stilled at last, they
        stand at the door,
    Watching the full-starred heavens that winter sees,
Will this thought rise on those who will meet my face
        no more,
    "He was one who had an eye for such mysteries"?

And will any say when my bell of quittance is heard in
        the gloom,
    And a crossing breeze cuts a pause in its outrollings,
Till they rise again, as they were a new bell's boom,
    "He hears it not now, but used to notice such
        things"?

THOMAS HARDY

Thrice Happy He

Thrice happy he, who by some shady grove,
Far from the clamorous world, doth live his own;
Though solitary, who is not alone,
But doth converse with that eternal love.
O how more sweet is birds' harmonious moan,
Or the soft sobbings of the widowed dove,
Than those smooth whisperings near a prince's
        throne,
Which good make doubtful, do the evil approve!
Or how more sweet is Zephyr's wholesome
        breath,
And sighs perfumed which do the flowers unfold,
Than that applause vain honor doth bequeath!
How sweet are streams to poison drunk in gold!
The world is full of horrors, falsehoods, slights;
Woods' silent shades have only true delights.

WILLIAM DRUMMOND

A Little Morning Music

The birds in the first light twitter and whistle,
Chirp and seek, sipping and chortling—weakly, meekly,
    they speak and bubble
As cheerful as the cherry would, if it could speak when
    it is cherry ripe or cherry ripening.
And all of them are melodious, erratic, and gratuitous,
Singing solely to heighten the sense of morning's
    beginning.
How soon the heart's cup overflows, how it is excited to
    delight and elation!

And in the first light, the cock's chant, roaring,
Bursts like rockets, rising and breaking into brief brilliance;
As the fields arise, cock after cock catches on fire,
And the pastures loom out of vague blue shadow,
The red barn and the red sheds rise and redden, blocks
    and boxes of slowly blooming wet redness;
Then the great awe and splendor of the sun comes nearer,
Kindling all things, consuming the forest of blackness,
    lifting and lighting up
All the darkling ones who slept and grew
Beneath the petals, the frost, the mystery and the
    mockery of the stars.
The darkened ones turn slightly in the faint light of the
    small morning,
Grow gray or glow green—
They are gray or green at once
        In the pale cool of blue light;
They dream of that other life and that otherness
Which is the darkness, going over
Maple and oak, leafy and rooted in the ancient and
    famous light,
In the bondage of the soil of the past and the radiance
    of the future.

But now the morning is growing, the sun is soaring, all
That lights up shows, quickly or slowly, the showing
    plenitude of fountains,
And soon an overflowing radiance, actual and dazzling,
    will braze and brim over all of us,
Discovering and uncovering all color and all kinds, all
    forms and all distances, rising and rising higher
  and higher, like a stupendous bonfire of
  consciousness,
Gazing and blazing, blessing and possessing all vividness
  and all darkness.

DELMORE SCHWARTZ

Proem

There is no rhyme that is half so sweet
As the song of the wind in the rippling wheat;
There is no meter that's half so fine
As the lilt of the brook under rock and vine;
And the loveliest lyric I ever heard
Was the wildwood strain of a forest bird.—
If the wind and the brook and the bird would teach
My heart their beautiful parts of speech,
And the natural art that they say these with,
My soul would sing of beauty and myth
In a rhyme and a meter that none before
Have sung in their love, or dreamed in their lore,
And the world would be richer one poet the more.

MADISON CAWEIN

from **The Signature of All Things**

When I dragged the rotten log
From the bottom of the pool,
It seemed heavy as stone.
I let it lie in the sun
For a month; and then chopped it
Into sections, and split them
For kindling, and spread them out
To dry some more. Late that night,
After reading for hours,
While moths rattled at the lamp—
The saints and the philosophers
On the destiny of man—
I went out on my cabin porch,
And looked up through the black forest
At the swaying islands of stars.
Suddenly I saw at my feet,
Spread on the floor of night, ingots
Of quivering phosphorescence,
And all about were scattered chips
Of pale cold light that was alive.

KENNETH REXROTH

from **Resolution and Independence**

I

There was a roaring in the wind all night;
The rain came heavily and fell in floods;
But now the sun is rising calm and bright;
The birds are singing in the distant woods;
Over his own sweet voice the Stock dove broods;
The Jay makes answer as the Magpie chatters;
And all the air is filled with pleasant noise of
    waters.

II

All things that love the sun are out of doors;
The sky rejoices in the morning's birth;
The grass is bright with raindrops;—on the moors
The hare is running races in her mirth;
And with her feet she from the plashy earth
Raises a mist, that, glittering in the sun,
Runs with her all the way, wherever she doth run.

WILLIAM WORDSWORTH

from **Hope**

My banks they are furnish'd with bees,
Whose murmur invites one to sleep;
My grottoes are shaded with trees,
And my hills are white over with sheep.
I seldom have met with a loss,
Such health do my fountains bestow;
My fountains all border'd with moss,
Where the harebells and violets grow.

Not a pine in the grove is there seen
But with tendrils of woodbine is bound;
Not a beech's more beautiful green
But a sweetbriar entwines it around:
Not my fields in the prime of the year,
More charms than my cattle unfold;
Not a brook that is limpid and clear,
But it glitters with fishes of gold.

WILLIAM SHENSTONE

Thanatopsis

To him who in the love of Nature holds
Communion with her visible forms, she speaks
A various language; for his gayer hours
She has a voice of gladness, and a smile
And eloquence of beauty, and she glides
Into his darker musings, with a mild
And healing sympathy, that steals away
Their sharpness ere he is aware. When thoughts
Of the last bitter hour come like a blight
Over thy spirit, and sad images
Of the stern agony, and shroud, and pall,
And breathless darkness, and the narrow house,
Make thee to shudder, and grow sick at heart;—
Go forth, under the open sky, and list
To Nature's teachings, while from all around—
Earth and her waters, and the depths of air,—
Comes a still voice—Yet a few days, and thee
The all-beholding sun shall see no more
In all his course; nor yet in the cold ground,
Where thy pale form was laid, with many tears,
Nor in the embrace of ocean, shall exist
Thy image. Earth, that nourished thee, shall claim
Thy growth, to be resolved to earth again,
And, lost each human trace, surrendering up
Thine individual being, shalt thou go
To mix for ever with the elements,
To be a brother to the insensible rock
And to the sluggish clod, which the rude swain
Turns with his share, and treads upon. The oak
Shall send his roots abroad, and pierce thy mold.

Yet not to thine eternal resting place
Shalt thou retire alone,—nor couldst thou wish
Couch more magnificent. Thou shalt lie down
With patriarchs of the infant world—with kings,

The powerful of the earth—the wise, the good,
Fair forms, and hoary seers of ages past,
All in one mighty sepulcher. The hills
Rock-ribbed and ancient as the sun; the vales
Stretching in pensive quietness between;
The venerable woods; rivers that move
In majesty, and the complaining brooks
That make the meadows green; and, poured
          round all,
Old ocean's gray and melancholy waste—
Are but the solemn decorations all
Of the great tomb of man. The golden sun,
The planets, all the infinite host of heaven,
Are shining on the sad abodes of death,
Through the still lapse of ages. All that tread
The globe are but a handful to the tribes
That slumber in its bosom.—Take the wings
Of morning, traverse Barca's desert sands,
Or lose thyself in the continuous woods
Where rolls the Oregon, and hears no sound,
Save his own dashings—yet—the dead are there:
And millions in those solitudes, since first
The flight of years began, have laid them down
In their last sleep—the dead reign there alone,
So shalt thou rest, and what if thou withdraw
In silence from the living, and no friend
Take note of thy departure? All that breathe
Will share thy destiny. The gay will laugh
When thou art gone, the solemn brood of care
Plod on, and each one as before will chase
His favorite phantom; yet all these shall leave
Their mirth and their employments, and shall come,
And make their bed with thee. As the long train
Of ages glides away, the sons of men,
The youth in life's green spring, and he who goes
In the full strength of years, matron, and maid,
And the sweet babe, and the gray-headed man—
Shall one by one be gathered to thy side,
By those, who in their turn shall follow them.

So live, that when thy summons comes to join
The innumerable caravan, which moves
To that mysterious realm, where each shall take
His chamber in the silent halls of death,
Thou go not, like the quarry slave at night,
Scourged to his dungeon, but, sustained and
      soothed
By an unfaltering trust, approach thy grave
Like one who wraps the drapery of his couch
About him, and lies down to pleasant dreams.

WILLIAM CULLEN BRYANT

The Ivy Green

O a dainty plant is the Ivy green,
    That creepeth o'er ruins old!
Of right choice food are his meals, I ween,
    In his cell so lone and cold.
The wall must be crumbled, the stone decayed,
    To pleasure his dainty whim;
And the moldering dust that years have made,
    Is a merry meal for him.
        Creeping where no Life is seen,
        A rare old plant is the Ivy green.

Fast stealeth he on, though he wears no wings,
    And a staunch old heart has he!
How closely he twineth, how tight he clings
    To his friend, the huge Oak Tree!
And slyly he traileth along the ground,
    And his leaves he gently waves,
As he joyously twines and hugs around
    The rich mold of dead men's graves.
        Creeping where grim Death has been,
        A rare old plant is the Ivy green.

Whole ages have fled, and their works decayed,
    And nations have scattered been;
But the stout old Ivy shall never fade
    From its hale and hearty green.
The brave old plant in its lonely days
    Shall fatten upon the past;
For the stateliest building man can raise
    Is the Ivy's food at last.
        Creeping on where Time has been,
        A rare old plant is the Ivy green.

CHARLES DICKENS

Root Cellar

Nothing would sleep in that cellar, dank as a
    ditch,
Bulbs broke out of boxes hunting for chinks in
    the dark,
Shoots dangled and drooped,
Lolling obscenely from mildewed crates,
Hung down long yellow evil necks, like tropical
    snakes.
And what a congress of stinks!—
Roots ripe as old bait,
Pulpy stems, rank, silo-rich,
Leaf mold, manure, lime, piled against slippery
    planks.
Nothing would give up life:
Even the dirt kept breathing a small breath.

THEODORE ROETHKE

Alpine

About mountains it is useless to argue,
You have either been up or you haven't;

The view from halfway is nobody's view.
The best flowers are mostly at the top

Under a ledge, nourished by wind.
A sense of smell is of less importance

Than a sense of balance, walking on clouds
Through holes in which you can see the earth

Like a rich man through the eye of a needle.
The mind has its own level to find.

R. S. THOMAS

The Two Deserts

Not greatly moved with awe am I
To learn that we may spy
Five thousand firmaments beyond our own.
The best that's known
Of the heavenly bodies does them credit small.
Viewed close, the Moon's fair ball
Is of ill objects worst,
A corpse in Night's highway, naked, fire-scarred, accurst;
And now they tell
That the Sun is plainly seen to boil and burst
Too horribly for hell.
So, judging from these two,
As we must do,
The Universe, outside our living Earth,
Was all conceived in the Creator's mirth,
Forecasting at the time Man's spirit deep,

To make dirt cheap.
Put by the Telescope!
Better without it man may see,
Stretched awful in the hushed midnight,
The ghost of his eternity.
Give me the nobler glass that swells to the eye
The things which near us lie,
Till Science rapturously hails,
In the minutest water drop,
A torment of innumerable tails.
These at the least do live.
But rather give
A mind not much to pry
Beyond our royal-fair estate
Betwixt these deserts blank of small and great.
Wonder and beauty our own courtiers are,
Pressing to catch our gaze,
And out of obvious ways
Ne'er wandering far.

COVENTRY PATMORE

Mountain Meadows

Mountain meadows is steep and narrow,
Thick with laurel and apple trees,
Berry bushes and rusted harrow,
Sugar maple and honey bees.

Pasture places is poor and scanty,
Rank with rubble and boulder stone—
Timothy by the logging shanty,
Fruit wherever a core were thrown.

Furrows tilts as the hill is tilted.
Mountain meadows is narrow land.
Over the brook the barn is builded,
Only place that a barn could stand.

Dwelling house is as black as pitch is.
Hemlock timbers is always black. . . .
Running water and roaring ditches,
Pine and popple and tamarack.

Mountain meadows is steep and stony,
Mountain waters is cold and strong—
Drawing me to the mortal-lonely
Mountain places where I belong.

Kettle Creek and Hailstone Hollow,
Burdick, Bunnel, and Elk Lick Run,
Cross Forks River and Hungry Hollow,
Windfall Water and Jamison. . . .

MARTHA KELLER

Mushrooms

Overnight, very
Whitely, discreetly,
Very quietly

Our toes, our noses
Take hold on the loam,
Acquire the air.

Nobody sees us,
Stops us, betrays us;
The small grains make room.

Soft fists insist on
Heaving the needles,
The leafy bedding,

Even the paving.
Our hammers, our rams,
Earless and eyeless,

Perfectly voiceless,
Widen the crannies,
Shoulder through holes. We

Diet on water,
On crumbs of shadow,
Bland-mannered, asking

Little or nothing.
So many of us!
So many of us!

We are shelves, we are
Tables, we are meek,
We are edible,

Nudgers and shovers
In spite of ourselves.
Our kind multiplies:

We shall by morning
Inherit the earth.
Our foot's in the door.

SYLVIA PLATH

Echo

You
Over there
Beyond the hill
Have nothing to say
Yet can't keep still—
Have nothing to do
But mimic me
And double the words
That I set free,
Garrulous ghost!
Garrulous ghost.

Maybe you'd say
In your defense
No echo practices
Reticence,
And the repartee
Of a voice's ghost
Makes conversation
As good as most!
As good as most.

MILDRED WESTON

Morels

A wet gray day—rain falling slowly, mist over the
    valley, mountains dark circumflex smudges in the
    distance—

Apple blossoms just gone by, the branches feathery still
    as if fluttering with half-visible antennae—

A day in May like so many in these green mountains, and
    I went out just as I had last year

At the same time, and found them there under the big
        maples—
    by the bend in the road—right where they had stood

Last year and the year before that, risen from the dark
        duff
    of the woods, emerging at odd angles

From spores hidden by curled and matted leaves, a
        fringe of
    rain on the grass around them,

Beads of rain on the mounded leaves and mosses round
    them,

Not in a ring themselves but ringed by jack-in-the-pulpits
    with deep eggplant-colored stripes;

Not ringed but rare, not gilled but polyp-like, having
    sprung up overnight—

These mushrooms of the gods, resembling human organs
    uprooted, rooted only on the air,

Looking like lungs wrenched from the human body,
        lungs
    reversed, not breathing internally

But being the externalization of breath itself, these
    spicy, twisted cones,

These perforated brown-white asparagus tips—these
        morels,
    smelling of wet graham crackers mixed with maple
        leaves;

And, reaching down by the pale green fern shoots, I
    nipped
    their pulpy stems at the base

And dropped them into a paper bag—a damp brown bag
    (their
    color)—and carried

Them (weighing absolutely nothing) down the hill and
    into
    the house; you held them

Under cold bubbling water and sliced them with a
    surgeon's
    stroke clean through,

And sautéed them over a low flame, butter-brown; and
    we ate
    them then and there—

Tasting of the sweet damp woods and of the rain one
    inch
    above the meadow:

It was like feasting upon air.

WILLIAM JAY SMITH

Times o' Year

    Here did sway the eltrot* flow'rs,
    When the hours o' night wer vew,
    An' the zun, wi' eärly beams
    Brighten'd streams, an' dried the dew,
    An' the goocoo there did greet
    Passers by wi' dousty veet.

* eltrot: *cow parsley*

There the milkmaïd hung her brow
By the cow, a-sheenèn red;
An' the dog, wi' upward looks,
Watch'd the rooks above his head,
An' the brook, vrom bow to bow,
Here went swift, an' there wer slow.

Now the cwolder-blowèn blast,
Here do cast vrom elems' heads
Feäded leaves, a-whirlèn round,
Down to ground, in yellow beds,
Ruslèn under milkers' shoes,
When the day do dry the dews.

Soon shall grass, a-vrosted bright,
Glisten white instead o' green,
An' the wind shall smite the cows,
Where the boughs be now their screen.
Things do change as years do vlee;
What ha' years in store vor me?

WILLIAM BARNES

To Turn Back

The grass people bow
their heads before the wind.

How would it be
to stand among them, bending
our heads like that . . . ?

Yes . . . and no . . . perhaps . . .
lifting our dusty faces
as if we were waiting for
the rain . . . ?

The grass people stand
all year, patient and obedient—

to be among them
is to have only simple
and friendly thoughts,

and not be afraid.

JOHN HAINES

Tumbleweed

Here comes another, bumping over the sage
Among the greasewood, wobbling diagonally
Downhill, then skimming a moment on its edge,
Tilting lopsided, bouncing end over end
And springing from the puffs of its own dust
To catch at the barbed wire
And hang there, shaking, like a riddled prisoner.

Half the sharp seeds have fallen from this tumbler,
Knocked out for good by head-stands and pratfalls
Between here and wherever it grew up.
I carry it in the wind across the road
To the other fence. It jerks in my hands,
Butts backward, corkscrews, lunges and swivels,
Then yaws away as soon as it's let go,
Hopping the scrub uphill like a kicked maverick.
The air goes hard and straight through the wires and
    weeds.
Here comes another, flopping among the sage.

DAVID WAGONER

The Seed Shop

Here in a quiet and dusty room they lie,
Faded as crumbled stone or shifting sand,
Forlorn as ashes, shriveled, scentless, dry—
Meadows and gardens running through my hand.

In this brown husk a dale of hawthorn dreams;
A cedar in this narrow cell is thrust
That will drink deeply of a century's streams;
These lilies shall make summer on my dust.

Here in their safe and simple house of death,
Sealed in their shells, a million roses leap;
Here I can blow a garden with my breath,
And in my hand a forest lies asleep.

MURIEL STUART

Nature

As a fond mother, when the day is o'er,
 Leads by the hand her little child to bed,
 Half willing, half reluctant to be led,
And leave his broken playthings on the floor,
Still gazing at them through the open door,
 Nor wholly reassured and comforted
 By promises of others in their stead,
Which, though more splendid, may not please
  him more;
So Nature deals with us, and takes away
 Our playthings one by one, and by the hand
  Leads us to rest so gently, that we go

Scarce knowing if we wish to go or stay,
　　Being too full of sleep to understand
　　　　How far the unknown transcends the what
　　we know.

HENRY WADSWORTH LONGFELLOW

Elegy for a Nature Poet

It was in October, a favorite season,
He went for his last walk. The covered bridge,
Most natural of all the works of reason,
Received him, let him go. Along the hedge

He rattled his stick; observed the blackening
　　bushes
In his familiar field; thought he espied
Late meadow larks; considered picking rushes
For a dry arrangement; returned home, and died

Of a catarrh caught in the autumn rains
And let go on uncared for. He was too rapt
In contemplation to recall that brains
Like his should not be kept too long uncapped

In the wet and cold weather. While we mourned,
We thought of his imprudence, and how Nature,
Whom he'd done so much for, had finally turned
Against her creature.

His gift was daily his delight, he peeled
The landscape back to show it was a story;
Any old bird or burning bush revealed
At his hands just another allegory.

Nothing too great, nothing too trivial
For him; from mountain range or humble vermin
He could extract the hidden parable—
If need be, crack the stone to get the sermon.

And now, poor man, he's gone. Without his name
The field reverts to wilderness again,
The rocks are silent, woods don't seem the same;
Demoralized small birds will fly insane.

Rude Nature, whom he loved to idealize
And would have wed, pretends she never heard
His voice at all, as, taken by surprise
At last, he goes to her without a word.

HOWARD NEMEROV

To the Sun

More beautiful than the remarkable moon and her noble
    light,
More beautiful than the stars, the famous medals of night,
Much more beautiful than the fiery entrance a comet
    makes,
And called to a part far more splendid than any other
    planet's
Because daily your life and my life depend on it, is the sun.

Beautiful sun that rises, his work not forgotten,
And completes it, most beautiful in summer, when a day
Evaporates on the coast, and effortlessly mirrored the sails
Pass through your sight, till you tire and cut short the last.

Without the sun even art takes the veil again,
You cease to appear to me, and the sea and the sand,
Lashed by shadows, take refuge under my eyelids.

Beautiful light, that keeps us warm, preserves us,
    marvelously makes sure
That I see again and that I see you again!

Nothing more beautiful under the sun than to be under
    the sun . . .

Nothing more beautiful than to see the stick in water
    and the bird above,
Pondering his flight, and, below, the fishes in shoals,

Colored, molded, brought into the world with a mission
    of light,
And to see the radius, the square of a field, my
    landscape's thousand angles

And the dress you have put on. And *your* dress, bell-
    shaped and blue!
Beautiful blue, in which peacocks walk and bow,

Blue of far places, the zones of joy with weathers that
    suit my mood,
Blue chance on the horizon! And my enchanted eyes
Dilate again and blink and burn themselves sore.

Beautiful sun, to whom dust owes great admiration yet,
Not for the moon, therefore, and not for the stars, and not

Because night shows off with comets, trying to fool me,
But for your sake, and endlessly soon, and for you above all

I shall lament the inevitable loss of my sight.

INGEBORG BACHMANN
Translated by Michael Hamburger

Give Me the Splendid Silent Sun

Give me the splendid silent sun with all his beams full-
    dazzling,
Give me juicy autumnal fruit ripe and red from the
    orchard,

Give me a field where the unmowed grass grows,
Give me an arbor, give me the trellised grape,
Give me fresh corn and wheat, give me serene-moving
    animals teaching content,
Give me nights perfectly quiet as on high plateaus west of
    the Mississippi, and I looking up at the stars,
Give me odorous at sunrise a garden of beautiful flowers
    where I can walk undisturbed,
Give me for marriage a sweet-breathed woman of whom
    I should never tire,
Give me a perfect child, give me away aside from the
    noise of the world a rural domestic life,
Give me to warble spontaneous songs recluse by myself,
    for my own ears only,
Give me solitude, give me Nature, give me again, O
    Nature, your primal sanities!

WALT WHITMAN

Looking Up at Leaves

No one need feel alone looking up at leaves.
There are such depths to them, withdrawal, welcome,
A fragile tumult on the way to sky.
This great trunk holds apart two hemispheres
We lie between . . . Like water lilies
Leaves fall, rise, waver, echoing
On their blue pool, whispering under the sun;
While in this shade, under our hands the brown
Tough roots seek down, lily roots searching
Down through their pool of earth to an equal depth.
Constant as water lilies we lie still,
Our breathing like the lapping of pond water,
Balanced between reflection and reflection.

BARBARA HOWES

Index of Authors

Index of Titles

ACKNOWLEDGMENTS

Acknowledgment is made to the following for permission to use material owned by them.

Ballantine Books, Inc., and Galway Kinnell, for "Spring Oak" by Galway Kinnell from *New Poems by American Poets*, edited by Rolfe Humphries, Copyright 1953 by Ballantine Books, Inc. Barrie Books Ltd., for "Weekend Stroll" from *On a Calm Shore* by Frances Cornford, Copyright © 1960 by Frances Cornford. "Village Before Sunset" from *Travelling Home* by Frances Cornford; published 1948. Robert Bly, for "Driving to Town Late to Mail a Letter," from *Silence in the Snowy Fields* by Robert Bly, published by Wesleyan University Press, 1962, Copyright 1962 by Robert Bly. Reprinted by permission of the author. Jonathan Cape Ltd. and The Estate of Muriel Stuart Board, for "The Seed Shop" from *Selected Poems* by Muriel Stuart. The Caxton Press, Christchurch, New Zealand, and Basil Dowling, for "Autumn Scene" from *Signs and Wonders* by Basil Dowling, Copyright 1944 by The Caxton Press. Chatto & Windus Ltd., for "The Full Heart" from *Ardours and Endurances* by Robert Nichols. Reprinted by permission of Mr. Milton Waldman and Chatto & Windus Ltd. The Clarendon Press, for "The Cliff-top," "The First Spring Morning," "The Idle Flowers," "London Snow," and "Spring Goeth All in White" by Robert Bridges. Reprinted from *Oxford Poetical Works* by permission of The Clarendon Press, Oxford. Collins-Knowlton-Wing, Inc., for "Star-talk," from *Over the Brazier* by Robert Graves. All rights reserved by Robert Graves. Reprinted by permission of Collins-Knowlton-Wing, Inc. Thomas Y. Crowell Company, for "Lobster Cove Shindig" from *The Ghost of Jersey City and Other Poems* by Lillian Morrison, Copyright © 1967 by Lillian Morrison. Reprinted by permission of the publishers, Thomas Y. Crowell Company, New York. Delacorte Press, for "The Morels" from *The Tin Can and Other Poems* by William Jay Smith, Copyright © 1966 by William Jay Smith. A Seymour Lawrence Book—Delacorte Press. Originally published in *The New Yorker*. Reprinted by permission. The Dolmen Press Ltd., for "A Strong Wind" from *Flight to Africa* by Austin Clarke, 1963. Doubleday & Company, Inc., for "Mid-country Blow," Copyright 1941 by Theodore Roethke, and "Root Cellar," Copyright 1943 by Modern Poetry Association, Inc., from *The Collected Poems of Theodore Roethke*. "A Little Morning Music," Copyright © 1959 by The New Yorker Magazine, Inc. (originally appeared in *The New Yorker*), and "The Deceptive Present, The Phoenix Year," Copyright © 1959 by Delmore Schwartz, from *Summer Knowledge* by Delmore Schwartz. All reprinted by permission of Doubleday & Company, Inc. Gerald Duckworth & Co., Ltd., for "In the Fields" and "The Trees Are Down" from *Collected Poems* by Charlotte Mew, Copyright 1953, © 1956 by Alida Monro. "Real Property" from *Collected Poems* by Harold Monro, Copyright 1933, © 1956 by Alida Monro. E. P. Dutton & Co., Inc., for "In Winter" from *Ungainly Things* by Robert Wallace, Copyright © 1968 by Robert Wallace. "In a Spring Still Not Written Of" from *Views from a Ferris Wheel* by Robert Wallace, Copyright © 1965 by Robert Wallace. "Giant Thunder" from *The Blackbird in the Lilac* by James Reeves, published 1959 by E. P. Dutton & Co., Inc., and reprinted with their permission. Norma Millay Ellis, for "The End of Summer" from *Renascence and Other Poems* by Edna St. Vincent Millay, published by Harper & Row, Publishers, Copyright 1917, 1944 by Edna St. Vincent Millay. Encounter Ltd., and John Cotton, for "Pumpkins" by John Cotton, Copyright © 1966 by Encounter Ltd. Mrs. Hazel Fetzer, for "Beautiful Sunday" from *The Bulls of Spring* by Jake Falstaff, Copyright 1937 by G. P. Putnam's Sons, renewed 1965 by Hazel Fetzer. Reprinted by permission of Mrs. Hazel Fetzer. Granada Publishing Limited, for "A Day in Autumn" from *Poetry for Supper* by R. S. Thomas, Copyright © 1958 by R. S. Thomas. "Farm Child" from *Song at the Year's Turning* by R. S. Thomas, Copyright © 1955 by R. S. Thomas. "Alpine" from *Tares* by R. S. Thomas, Copyright © 1961 by R. S. Thomas. "The Fallen Tree," "The Beech," "Snow Harvest," and "Hard Frost" from *Collected Poems* by Andrew Young, Copyright © 1960 by Andrew Young. All published by Rupert Hart-Davis. Harcourt, Brace & World, Inc., for "Seed Leaves," from *Walking to Sleep* by Richard Wilbur, Copyright © 1964 by Richard Wilbur. First published in *The New Yorker*. "Exeunt" from *Things of This World* by Richard Wilbur, Copyright 1952 by The New Yorker Magazine, Inc. "when faces called flowers float out of the ground" from *Poems 1923–1954* by E. E. Cummings, Copyright 1950 by E. E. Cummings. "Lives" from *A Map of Verona and Other Poems* by Henry Reed, Copyright 1947 by Henry Reed. "Let us Go, Then, Exploring," from